Black Rose

Black Rose

Jennifer Ceballos

Library of Congress Control Number:		2011962244
ISBN:	Hardcover	978-1-4691-3414-7
	Softcover	978-1-4691-3413-0
	Ebook	978-1-4691-3415-4

This book was printed in the United States of America.

To order additional copies of this book, contact:
Xlibris Corporation
1-888-795-4274
www.Xlibris.com
Orders@Xlibris.com
107294

Contents

Preface 9

The Beginning and the End 11

Death 24

Chemistry 26

Ravendell Mall 30

Confession 37

Realization 41

Saturday 49

Black Rose 52

Blur 55

Intruder 60

Tyler Dawson 70

The Drive Home 78

Dream 87

The Whole Truth 92

Questions 96

Sun Rise 108

Confrontation 115

The River 119

Not My Time 121

Alone 125

The Funeral 130

Dedication Page

I want to dedicate this book to my Parents for whom I thank for letting me read all kinds of books, and to my sisters for keeping me motivated to keep writing. Also to a select few of my friends I thank for sticking around you know who you are if it wasn't for you guys I wouldn't have been able to finish this book. I also want to thank Forrest who encouraged me to keep going when things got a little rough.

For
My wonderful Family
To
David and Michelle Cutlip

Preface

Swish! Swish!

"Higher Mommy!" The wind flew through my hair as I swung on my newly made rope swing I could feel my cheeks turn red with excitement. Daddy said it was dangerous for a seven year old to be swinging on a homemade swing, but Mommy came back with, 'it's all part of a child's life to make home made things as parents we shouldn't interfere with a growing free spirit, and making a homemade swing is all part of little Anne's spirit.'

"My little Anne any higher and you'll be touching the heavens!" I giggled in response to that.

"I can't touch the heavens Mommy, I'm still alive!"

"That's right sweetie!" Mommy grabbed me before I swung forward.

I could hear Mommy laughing, "You are so smart my little one."

Before I knew it I was in her arms as her long black hair brushed my cheek, I could smell the sweet fragrance of flowers.

"I'm smart like you Mommy." as we hugged I planted a kiss on her soft cheek.

"You are smart just like Mommy." I smiled, I was so happy.

"Are you ready to get back on the swing my little Anne?"

"Yes Mommy!" I was giggling as Mommy put me back on the swing—I waited for her to push me, but there was nothing.

"Mommy?" I turned around and I saw her laying on the ground she wasn't moving—I quickly got off the swing and knelt down next to her. Her face looked pale a little sweat was gathering on her forehead—I brushed my hand across her cheek it felt warm to the touch I didn't know if that was normal or not.

"Mommy?" Her eye's opened a little.

"Go get Daddy sweetie." Her voice sounded hoarse and I began to feel scared. "Go Anne." I ran to the porch and opened the screen door.

"Daddy something's wrong with Mommy!" I quickly ran down the porch stairs tripping on the last one causing myself to land on both my knee's I scraped them that was for sure, but I couldn't take any time worrying about that. I got up and ran to her I could feel tears running down my cheeks—I knelt back down and placed my small hand into her hand.

"Don't cry sweetie everything is going to be okay." She lifted her other hand and brushed away the tears from my cheek—Daddy was by my side in no time breathing heavily.

"Ambulance is on the way honey." I moved to the side allowing Daddy to pull Mommy into his arms. I looked at Daddy then back to Mommy.

"Don't touch the heavens Mommy!" I didn't mean to cry it out, but I couldn't help it I was scared, and it was the first thing that flew out of my lips—she grabbed my hand.

"You are so smart my little one." I held on tighter to her hand.

"Like you Mommy." A shutter escaped my lips and more tears ran down my face.

"That's right sweetie just like Mommy . . . ."

The Beginning and the End

All around people were pushing each other trying to move the line a little faster. I didn't feel right going to this stupid concert, but Dad insisted that I should have time for myself and have a little fun 'It's not normal for a young girl to stress so much about grown up problems'. I hardly thought Mom having leukemia was 'just a grown up problem', but I caved and decided to go unwillingly. I had a feeling Tammy and Tyler were not going to give me a chance to bail out.

"Hey you going to try to smile, or are you just going to look like your puppy got run over by a car?" Tyler was staring at me with a critical look on his face.

"I'm just thinking that's all Tyler." I crossed my arms over my chest and tried to ignore him.

"Looks like some serious thinking Anne." Tyler grabbed me by the arm and dragged me to the front giving the guy our tickets and ran me into the crowds of young angsty teens to see a heavy metal rock band that I really didn't care for, but for Tyler's sake I was going to humor him for the next three or four hours. I was going to punch the crap out of Tammy later for bailing out on me—she came up with some lame ass excuse about having to help her Mom with some dress crap at the shop. Lies lies lies!, but no matter what Tammy was and will always be my best friend no matter how many times she bailed out on me.

Tyler still had me by the arm trying to get us the best view lucky enough the concert was outside I couldn't stand the smell of toxic smoke coming from groups of rather high teenagers the smell bothered me I tried to ignore the massive headache creeping up the back of my neck. I was miserable and annoyed, but I had to make sure that I looked like I was having fun I really didn't want Tyler getting onto me every minute. Tyler finally got us to the middle of the crowed I was still way too deep in thought to even pay attention as to what was going on.

"Trust me I'm going to get us to that stage even if I have to start hurting people." Tyler was dedicated I would give him that. "Just try not to hurt me in the process Tyler."

"Ya right your safe with me Anne." Tyler pulled at my arm again and started for the hunt of getting us through this crowed and too the front of the stage. By the time I thought my arm was going to be pulled out of its socket he managed to push through the last row of people. "Oh thank god Tyler . . . . I think my arm was about to say fare well to my shoulder."

"Sorry Anne didn't mean to drag you around. Tyler was smiling and breathing a little heavily. But hey—here's the stage lets enjoy the fact that I got us here." An hour passed I kept looking down at my phone, I wasn't really too interested in paying attention.

One of the bands sucked real bad I didn't really give a crap what the name of the band was I didn't want to remember that god awful performance. Tyler's taste in music was a little interesting at times I couldn't understand it—deep growling so called singing and really loud drumming—but he loved it for some reason. Me and Mom always talked about Tyler and his music and how passionate he talked about his heavy metal—we would just sit back and listen to his none stop rants about how many people confused a lot of bands as heavy metal, but now I didn't have anyone to talk about those things too—my mom was so sick sometimes she couldn't even have long conversations with me. Half the time she couldn't even wake up she looked so frail. The hospital bed was her own personal hell or so I thought.

"You know this is a concert right?" I was yanked back into the loud music and Tyler's loud voice. Tyler was looking at me with complete confusion on his face he didn't really understand my never ending want to be so down on life.

"Ya I know what it is Tyler . . . . I'm just way to distracted right now and I just can't get into this . . . . I just can't help but think about my mom . . . I mean I'm out here having 'fun' while she's in a hospital bed getting constantly poked by doctors and throwing up what little food she has in her . . . so ya try having 'fun' with that on your mind."

Tyler was shaking his head in disapproval.

"Anne just let your mind rest for a while—Mrs. Black is about the most toughest women I've ever known and I'm sure your Mom will understand that you're taking a break from this very dark moment in you're life—so let's just have a little fucking fun for once in you're damn life Anne . . . take it easy on being depressed it's really starting to rub off on me Anne and I'm the one who's supposed to help you get better—what would be the point of helping you out when I'm depressed." Tyler put his arm around my shoulder and gave me a little a hug.

The crowed began to cheer as a another band walked onto the stage—people were pushing us against the stage I didn't like the feeling of having so many people this close to me—"My Dying Bride" seemed to be a favorite amongst the massive crowed the song started off really mellow with a long piano solo slowly after a drum beat followed suit. Everyone was swaying to the song—The lead singer opened his mouth and mournfully sung out '*Can everybody see you've got a war to fight*'—a mournful violin joined in it was beginning to get to my heart I was beginning to feel alone I wasn't sure why I was feeling this way. I put my hand to my chest, but it didn't seem to help. The drumming continued and the piano followed slowly behind.

I could feel the heat of everyone behind me, and the swaying of everyone's bodies began to annoy me I lowered my head a little and put my hand to my forehead. I wanted more than anything for it to be over for him to stop singing in such a way that made me want to cry. I wanted to leave to push my body through the crowds and run from this place. I could feel a strong grip on my shoulder I looked up and Tyler was staring at me.

"What is it Anne . . . . what's wrong?" Tyler ran his first finger gently up my cheek.

"I—I . . . . couldn't seem to get the words out. I didn't know why Tyler was touching my face.

"Anne you're crying . . . . Tyler moved his hand to the other side of my face and gently wiped away more tears that I had no idea were running down my face. I stopped him from wiping away more from my face.

"Tyler I want to go home . . . . I don't feel right." Tyler gently put his hand into mine.

"You don't have to explain Anne." And with that Tyler started to walk me through the swaying crowds of young teens. The faces became blurry and it was then that more tears began to fill my eye's—I tried blinking them away, but it didn't seem to want to stop. Tyler began to wipe more tears away from my face—It was strange how Tyler wouldn't shy away from a crying girl.

"Don't worry Anne I'm going to get you home." We finally made it to Tyler's car—he opened the passenger door for me—I slide in and the door closed slowly after. I laid my head on the window, and closed my eyes. I could feel Tyler getting in the driver's side I was starting to feel bad for ending the night like this.

"I'm so sorry . . .

I could hear Tyler shifting in his seat, but I didn't hear him slide his key into the ignition.

"Don't be sorry Anne . . . .

He placed his hand on my shoulder. "Look at me Anne." I didn't want too I was ashamed of myself, but I couldn't help it. Tyler moved closer and placed his hand under my chin and gently moved my face towards him. It made me feel very nervous that Tyler was this close to me.

"I understand . . . . Don't feel bad—okay just relax and I'll be sure you make it home safely." I nodded my head—Tyler wiped away one remaining tear from my face and with that he slide his key into the ignition and drove out of the parking lot.

Rain began pattering against the window on my side—I didn't know why things turned out this way—I looked up at the sky the clouds had a blackish look too them and for some reason I felt that in my heart something was wrong. I wanted to get home as soon as possible to make sure I was just being paranoid and tense for no reason. I was nervous I kept biting my bottom lip and I could taste a little blood kind of gross but I didn't care.

I looked at Tyler and he glanced at me for a second.

"Honestly Anne you really need to stop doing that."

"I can't help it I'm nervous for some damn reason." I could feel my heart beating a little harder than usual I was beginning to feel chills run up my spine and I began to shiver. My teeth chattered I didn't feel cold, but something was causing me to feel really off.

"What's up with you Anne." I could hear the concern in Tyler's voice. I looked at him and he seemed to be confused as well.

"I'm not sure Tyler I just feel . . . . ugh! I can't seem to explain it. Maybe I should call my Dad." I grabbed my cell phone out of my back pocket and dialed my Dad's number. It rang a couple of times and went to voice mail—I didn't bother leaving one. I lowered my head into my hands and rubbed my eye's I didn't care that I might have wrecked my eye makeup.

"We're almost there Anne." Tyler was speeding a little, but at this point I really didn't care, his car was meant to get you anywhere quick Tyler loved his car I couldn't really blame him it was a very nice sleek black 1967 Chevy Impala no one could drive that car but him. I looked out the window and I could see my neighborhood in the distance.

"I hope I'm freaking out for nothing Tyler because I don't really like the way I'm feeling. Please tell me I'm going crazy for nothing Tyler." I turned to look at him, he was leaning into his stirring wheel Tyler seemed to be concentrating really hard. He breathed out a little and looked at me.

"I wouldn't even begin to tell you how you should be feeling Anne—not in this situation it's to difficult to say anything really, but i think you should breathe a little . . . you look like you're about to pass out. Tyler placed a hand on my shoulder and pushed me back so I was completely lying back in the seat. "Just breath for me okay Anne." I nodded and let a little air out of my lungs. Tyler pulled up to the street I lived on it was a quiet town not much went on everyone seemed to be nice on most days. Tyler parked in front of my house one light seemed to be on I was praying to god that everything was okay. I yanked the car door opened and slide out of the Impala. I rested my hand on the car door before closing it.

"You want me to come in with you Anne?" Tyler was leaning closer to the passenger seat. I bent down to look at Tyler. "Maybe you should wait here Tyler I think I'll go in and check it out first and if I need you then I'll call you.

"Alright I'll wait." Tyler turned off his car and leaned back into his seat. I closed the car door gently so as not to wake any of the neighbors I checked my phone it was going on midnight the walk way to my house had tiny rocks that would crackle under any pressure it was Dad's idea to make a rocky walk way he said it would be different from the other walk ways in the neighborhood. I made it to the door and put my hand on it, I wasn't sure what I was doing—maybe I was trying to get some kind of reading off of it—maybe touching part of the house would let me know if something bad was happening, but all I could feel was how cold the wood felt under my fingers. I turned around I could see Tyler lighting up a cigarette the flash of the light lit up his face I could see the rugged angles of his face—I wondered if he was staring at me wondering why I was just standing here. I turned around and breathed out a little air to catch my bearings—I dug my key out of my bag and with shaking hands unlocked the door I waited for a second my shoulders tensed up a little finally I pushed the door opened. Reluctantly I walked in I placed my bag on the floor and I walked into the living room the lights were left on in the kitchen I looked at the stairs leading up to the bedrooms my gaze went back to the kitchen and then back to the stairs I was hoping Dad would walk down them at any moment, but he didn't. I looked at the stairs for a little while longer, but still nothing my heart sank. The small dining room was barely visible by the kitchen light—I walked closer to the dining room table and noticed a white piece of paper I scrambled to the table and snatched the note I thought at any moment I would rip it in two by the way I was griping the small note I could tell this was rushed my Dads hand writing looked panicked.

I needed to head to the hospital Anne . . . . I'm sorry I
I had to leave without giving you a call. I'll explain
everything once you get to the hospital.
—Love Dad

I felt scared I didn't know what to do—this wasn't good at all—The fear of losing my Mom always came to my mind, but I just didn't think something like this would happen so soon. I was stuck to the floor I couldn't get my legs too move I was glued to this spot. I felt slight pressure on my shoulder—I managed to move my head Tyler was looking at me with concern again.

"What's up Anne?" I couldn't speak not one word would come out. Tyler grabbed the note out of my hand and looked at it for a moment his face was serious.

"Well what are you waiting for Anne lets go to the hospital." Tyler grabbed my arm and we both ran out of my house and into Tyler's car. Tyler speed out of the street like a bat out of hell.

We got to Revendall hospital in two hours it would have taken three, but lucky for me Tyler broke a couple of speeding laws and ran a few stop signs. The rain began to come down harder, but it didn't seem to faze Tyler one bit. Tyler parked his car in the visitors parking section. I could feel the headache coming on I felt like my head was going to split apart—I was scared I didn't know what the Doctor was going to say to me—I didn't know Moms' Doctor very well I think his name was David I never really had a chance to speak to him, I saw him a couple of times from a distance I never really had a chance to get a good look at him. Tyler opened the passenger side door for me and like a zombie I got out of the car slowly. "You're not going to pass out on me are you Anne?"

"No I'm fine Tyler . . .

Entering the hospital was always hard for me it was always an everyday thing for me and my Dad. It smelled weird it always made me feel uncomfortable, but I was always there for my Mom and I was but today felt different it felt sad. Me and Tyler walked around the hospital for a while—took a couple of elevators got lost twice and nearly walked into somebody else's room until we found the right hallway. Tyler was close by my side I felt safe to have Tyler here with me. I looked up to see my Dad sitting outside of my Mom's room he looked like he rolled right out of bed not worrying about how he looked to the public. Tyler touched my shoulder I looked up at him his face looked sadden.

"Go find out what's up Anne—I'll be right here." I nodded and walked to my Dad.

I placed my hand on my Dad's shoulder he looked up at me his eyes looked red and tired.

"Oh hi honey; I'm glad you could make it." I was worried I didn't know what he was going to tell me.

"I came as soon as I got the note—Tyler brought me." Dad looked behind me and saw Tyler standing against the wall. "Hello Tyler—thanks for bringing Anne means a lot."

"No Problem Mr. Black." Tyler had a slight smile on his face.

"So is Mom okay?" I wasn't sure if I was ready for the answer.

"I don't think it looks very good Anne she's strong, but . . . Dad paused for a moment it looked like he wanted to cry—I could see the pain in his eye's and it was breaking my heart. He took in a breath and cleared his throat and continued on.

"This could possibly be the last night she can hold on too." I wanted to protest to yell until I couldn't anymore, but for some reason I couldn't get myself to do it. Dad continued to talk and he was rubbing his eyes in frustration. I knew it hurt him too tell me this.

"The Doctors say that her body is refusing the Chemotherapy I think she wants it to be over as well . . ." I finally found my voice.

"Wait . . . No . . . don't say that, Mom has to be okay there's no way . . . . I'm not going to accept that!"

"Honey . . . I now you don't want to hear this, but she says she's done fighting."

My heart just dropped right then and there I felt my face go very pale. I could hear Tyler walking up behind me—everything went muffled I couldn't hear what Tyler was saying—but next thing I knew I was moving.

The only thing I remembered was pushing the door open to my Mom's room. There she was lying there in her hospital bed she looked worse from my last visit she looked skinner and paler.

The whole thing made me feel like I was in a horrible nightmare, and it made me feel like a child again, I wasn't sure, but I think I was crying and whispering Mommy like I was four again. I saw her head move she was looking at me with her beautiful blue eyes; I remember how she looked at me . . . . like I was her everything and that I was the only thing in her world that she loved. Mom smiled a bit and I knew that took a lot of strength for her to do that—she lifted her small hand. I walked towards her it was like I was walking in slow motion, and that the world was falling on top of me I tried to smile, but it was a complete disaster, so I just looked down at my boots. "Come to me Anne." she said lightly it was like God himself was calling me to heaven—more like hell if you know what I mean. I felt my chest go tight I could barely breathe it was like my chest was trying to eat my heart. "Don't be scared honey, come . . . please sit down."

I finally made it to her bed I sat down on the edge of her bed, and kept staring at my boots. As much as I could muster up I put my hand in her hand it felt soft. "Please look at me Anne." I looked up as slowly as I could, I was afraid to see what was there. My eyes connected to her eyes.

"You look so good Anne . . . look at you so grown up—your Father told me you went to a concert.

"Ya—I went with Tyler to this 'Metal Mosh Event' it was crazy." I didn't want to cry I was trying really hard to hold it in.

"That's good I'm glad you're taking some time to have a little fun Anne—you need that . . . Let's see what you're wearing I'm always interested in what you kids wear these days." I got up to and let her look at me. "I love it . . . it's so interesting." Mom smiled and gave a slight pat on her bed—I sat back down.

"I'm sorry—I didn't get a chance to change—I must look really odd walking in here with boots, my crazy tight black chain pants, and this crazy shirt. I laughed a little—Tyler is here with me too he's dressed up as crazy as I am."

"That boy is something Anne, but he's a good guy." Mom smiled at that. I nodded and looked down at my boots again. My bangs fell to my face it was the only long part of my hair the rest was cut short in layers. I took in a breath and waited for the next thing Mom would say—I knew that the small talk would have to end—and that the conversation would turn into a serious one. Mom moved my bangs from my face and I knew it was coming.

"Anne I know you're scared right now, but you need to be strong for me and you're Father, you know he is doing his best to take care of you while I'm here."

"Mom please don't talk like this I don't think I can bare it."

"I know Anne . . . . but you know I need to tell you this, because I don't want you to feel like you can't live without me, your Father is a wonderful man, and I have great trust in him." I moved my other hand into her hand.

"Please . . . I can't hear this Mom its hurting me too much." A tear ran down my cheek I knew I couldn't hold it in anymore.

"Just listen to me honey . . . I'm not going to last much longer, and you need to be strong . . . for me . . . please Anne." It wasn't fair I didn't understand why she had to be the one to go.

"Please! Don't leave me . . . oh God!" I covered my face with my hands.

"You can do this I know you can, you're a strong young lady Anne."

I know I was being spoiled, but she was my Mom, any person would react like this—anyone normal at least.

Mom grabbed my arm and pulled me closer to her. I put my arms around my Mom and hugged her, so that death couldn't get his filthy fingers all over her. "It's all right Anne, I'll always be watching over you, you know that."

"No you can't leave me I'll hate you if you did." I could feel my Moms body go ridged I could tell that it hurt her to hear me say that, I started crying, I wanted to tell Mom that I didn't mean it, but I heard the door open behind me. "Hi" I glanced behind me to see who interrupted my moment with my Mom, "Oh hi David I'm just talking to my daughter." I was confused—this was Mom's Doctor, I didn't understand he looked way too young to be a Doctor I couldn't look away from him. My eyeliner was probably messed up from crying, and I probably looked crazy I wasn't really dressed for a hospital visit—but it didn't really look like he cared.

"Um . . . Anne right, I heard so much about you, my name is David I've been taking care of your Mom."

David walked up to me, he had the most pricing green eyes almost the color of emerald; it threw me off I never knew anyone with eye's such as his. I kind of gasped, (I now a bit embarrassing). Like an idiot I didn't realize that David was holding up his hand, I shook my head and placed my hand into his, the greeting was over in a second, I was confused to the fact that this simple touch tingled my skin and sent chills down my spine. David walked passed me and went to my Mom's bedside.

"How are you feeling Mrs. Black?

"I'm feeling well." Mom said softly. I stopped staring at my hand and looked at both David and my Mom—David was checking her vitals and having a simple conversation with my Mom as if nothing bad was going to happen to her. I couldn't help feeling as if everybody was going crazy; did no one know that my Mom was going to die at any moment? "Well everything seems to be in order; I'm going to make sure everything is comfortable for you Mrs. Black."

"Oh thank you David it's very much appreciated; you've been really kind to me for these many grueling months."

"You're welcome Mrs. Black—I'm happy that I transferred to this hospital to get a chance to meet you and take care of you—it's been a pleasure."

I couldn't take it anymore, I started backing away slowly Mom noticed the movement and looked my way. "Anne where are you going I still need to talk to you." I shook my head in disbelief.

Right then and there I turned and ran away as fast as my boots would allow I could hear the loud clunking noise as I ran—other nurses and Doctors stared as I ran pass them—I heard someone say something, but I wasn't too sure what it was. Tears were flowing from my eyes it didn't feel like they would stop. Everyone was acting so calm and it was way too weird for me and unfair, it was like they felt death was a normal thing. I looked behind me it didn't even look like anyone bothered chasing after me, not even Tyler. I looked ahead to concentrate at what was in front of me, I really didn't want to bump into anything or anyone. All of a sudden I felt someone grab my arm, I thought maybe it was Tyler I tried to tug my arm away from him. "Just stop!" That wasn't Tyler's voice I knew that for sure. I couldn't believe that David stopped me I didn't know why he was the one who chased after me I wasn't expecting that. I stared at him and I'm pretty sure I had this really confused look on my face.

"Why . . . did . . .

"Listen to me, you need to go back to your Mom she's dying, and her wish is to see you before that happens." David was looking straight into my eyes, it made me nervous.

"I can't . . .

"Yes you can."

This was so weird—last time I checked Doctors never really made the habit of chasing their patient's family members down.

"You need to go back now—you're Mom loves you . . . I can see that and she's just trying to make things right Anne." It made me uncomfortable that David said my name so easily in such a serious moment. David still had a hold of my arm and it was starting to hurt, I tried to pry his hand off my arm, but he was too strong.

"Please let me go you're starting to hurt me."

"Oh . . . right . . . sorry." David let go of me and backed away a few paces. It was silent for a moment—I decided to break the silence first. "I'll go back . . . . but on one condition you have to stay outside the room." David looked at me and agreed quickly.

"All right then I will, but if you need anything call me right away." I was really confused, and I wasn't too sure what had just happened, but me and David walked back the way I came—I decided to ask a question.

"Why don't you introduce yourself formally . . . . you know how most Doctors do?" David looked at me and seemed to decide that it was safe to talk about this topic.

"Well I don't like throwing my title around, and most people call me David anyway, Plus if I went for the formal stuff it would make me feel old, and I don't like that idea."

"Well, you're not that old looking, to me; you look quite young to be a Doctor."

"Well, one tries." David smiled at me. I felt something happen to my heart I kept getting this odd feeling about him, when I touched his hand it was like I had some strange connection to him—I couldn't explain it, but there had to be a logical explanation. "Here we are." I was brought back from my thoughts and looked up to see that I was right at the door of my Mom's room. I drew in a breath and turned to face David.

"Okay . . . . all I need for you to do is stay out here in the hallway." I turned towards my Mom's room, but just as I was about to go in David grabbed my arm. I looked up at him.

"Please talk with her . . . you have to know she has little time left."

I couldn't help but get that feeling again I didn't understand what it all meant, and David's eyes weren't helping much either.

"She's my Mom—I know what I'm going to say . . . . I think." I didn't feel confident.

David let go of my arm—walked to the door and opened it for me. I walked up to the entrance and stopped.

"Thank you for taking care of my Mom David." David looked at me didn't say anything, but he just stared at me for a while it seemed that there was recognition in his eyes, but it slowly faded away—he gave a nod of his head and smiled.

David backed away to the farthest part of the hallway—Tyler walked up with two cups in his hands I guess that explained why he didn't come after me I looked at his face it was filled with anger I wasn't sure why—I tried to ignore it I would ask him later about it. I took a breath in and walked into the hospital room closing the door behind me. I didn't want to turn around but I knew I had to face her I spun around slowly—Dad was sitting in the chair that was next to the bed. I stared at my Mom and Dad for a while; I remembered how happy they were, but now there they were with the saddest looks on their faces. Dad looked up and for a moment my heart just sunk for him.

"Oh . . . Hi honey, how are you feeling?" Dad smiled the best smile he could muster up.

"Under the circumstances . . . fine I guess." I shrugged my shoulders as I said this.

"I'll be out in the hall if you need me." Dad got up from his chair kissed Mom on the forehead ever so lightly, and before he left he gave me a kiss on the top of my head. "Hang in there kiddo." And with that the door closed behind him. I looked down at the floor I was ashamed for running like I did.

"I'm sorry; I shouldn't have run away like that."

"I understand you were just scared, if I were in your shoes I'd probably do the same thing honey." I walked to the chair Dad was sitting in and sat down I stared at Mom for a while.

A sigh escaped my lips and my whole body seemed to slump over.

"I love you mom . . . I don't think I said it that often." I felt my heart ache.

"Oh honey you didn't have to say it, I saw it in your eyes every day, even when you were mad at me." The thing was, I didn't want to lose my Mom, and in some cases Mom was a huge part of my life.

I couldn't stand it anymore, I got up and laid down with her, I gave her a kiss on her soft cheek and just put my arms around her. I laid there and I couldn't bring myself to say anything.

"I Love you Anne." There was this sound I couldn't understand, and then I realized what it was—a flat line.

"Mom?" there was nothing I looked up and she wasn't breathing no life seemed to be in her eye's the light was gone from them, I didn't know what to do, I grabbed her and pulled her into my arms I could feel tears rolling down my cheeks all the sounds in the room became muffled.

"No . . . . comeback you can't leave me here . . . please I can't lose you Mom . . . . wake up! The door to my Moms' room flew open—I cried out and held my Mom closer to me. Tyler knelt down in front of me.

"Anne you have to let her go." Tyler grabbed my arm.

"No I won't let her go Tyler!

"You have to Anne." Tyler pulled at my arm again.

"No . . . . please Tyler . . . please." My voice became a whisper and I could see Tyler eyes become filled with sadness. I looked up from Tyler—David was standing in the doorway Dad was standing behind him and I could tell Dad was crying. David walked to my side and knelt down next to Tyler.

"Anne I know this is difficult for you, but I have to . . . .

"No you can't! Why isn't anyone helping her . . . . please bring her back!" I felt my heart weakening . . . there was so much hurt running through me I didn't know what to do. A nurse walked in and turned off the heart monitor.

"David I have to have this room empty . . . .

"Just give us a moment Elizabeth I'm working on it." David shot the nurse a stern look she jumped and walked out of the room as fast as possible. David turned his attention to me and his eyes became soft and clear.

"You have to let your Mom go Anne."

Death

The cause of death was death. Death is a funny thing if you think about it; I mean you try to keep it away, but just when you think death won't get you he pulls a surprising trick on you and pulls you right in. That's what death did to my Mom and I thought that was a bunch of bullshit if you asked me. Death made me sick to my stomach it made me feel cold inside, it trapped me in like a helpless bug. Death is an enemy not a friend people always tell me death is a good thing, but it isn't it's a curse it causes extreme sorrow and suffering. Why in the world would anyone hope for such a thing?

I really didn't remember going to the funeral, there were things I did remember, I remembered how beautiful she looked, and it was kind of disturbing she looked like a ghost. I also remembered David he looked sad, I remember him looking up at me he caught my eyes, I couldn't look away it was like there was a pull that I couldn't explain. I ignored it as best as possible.

The memory of the hospital popped into my head. Everyone ran into the room—I was holding my Mom and crying very loudly—I didn't want to let her go—Tyler grabbed my arms but I wouldn't let him pull me away from Mom, and then David came in and grabbed me he did what others couldn't—he pulled me away from my Mom—I cried out and tears flowed out of my eyes, my boots smacked the floor, and in one swoop Tyler pulled me away from David and pulled me up into his arms and carried me out of my Mom's room. I shook the memory out of my head, the ride home was quiet and when we pulled up to the house I didn't wait for my Dad I just walked to the door—let myself in—didn't care to look around walked up to the stairs—dragged myself up them and into my room closing the door behind me.

I closed all the curtains so the light of the sun wouldn't come in—I tossed my shoes off and took my black dress off I crawled into my bed and went under my blankets hoping this would help hide me from the world. I don't know why but the dark always made me feel at piece maybe that's how my Mom felt in her dark abyss I felt like yelling and screaming I couldn't believe that the very thing I loved was taken away from me. I cried all night until I fell asleep

For some odd reason my dreams were filled with David he looked so beautiful—in way he looked like an angel and every part of me wanted to be with him, but the dream changed into something awful. I felt like I was trapped and I was trying my hardest to find my way out. I heard crying and I didn't know where it was coming from—I was walking in what seemed like a dark corridor it was hard to find my way—the girls cries seemed to get louder I made it to a room and saw that a girl was sitting on the floor her back was facing towards me—I was kind of scared, but at the same time the dream felt so familiar I didn't know why I felt that way. As I walked up to the girl I saw my own arm extend and touch her shoulder—she turned around so fast that I fell down flat on my back it took me a moment to sit up, but when I finally did I saw her face, I couldn't believe what I was seeing it was me only I looked different. She had long black hair some of which was falling to her face she was dressed in an old fashioned dress, and she was crying she looked like she was in so much pain. She extended her hand out it was full of blood.

I could tell there was a large amount of blood coming from her stomach—and at that very moment I felt death I could hear someone yelling beside me, but I couldn't tell who it was. The dream was fading and I woke up screaming.

Chemistry

Two Months Later

I had a really bad headache, school wasn't a big help. I felt like I couldn't go on any more people were just too loud and I just wanted a little piece and quiet. Two months had passed, and fall break was just around the corner—everyone was ready for the Autumn dance you could see the smiles on girls faces, they were more than ready to get started. Me on the other hand I didn't feel anything for dances I saw it as a pointless thing, for some reason the Autumn dance was a big deal in Ravendell bigger then Prom I really didn't understand it. I wanted more than anything to just go home and go to bed where I could just be alone, but Dad was trying to put an end of me spending my days in my bed.

I walked into chemistry class not wanting to do a damn thing. Everyone kept staring at me knowing I was the girl with the dead Mom. I wanted to punch people in their faces for staring at me that way—if there was one thing I hated it was pity and snoops. Not many of the teenagers I was surrounded by didn't even know me until now—heck some of them were really rude to me before—I sat down in my usual spot to listen to Mr. Robert drone on about problems no one even cared about. I laid my head down on the desk to try to drown out some of the things Mr. Robert was talking about, until I felt someone tap my shoulder. I didn't even want to lift up my head to acknowledge the person that was tapping my shoulder.

"What?" I said it with as much enthusiasm as possible—which was not much.

"Hey Anne . . . . how's it going?" Me and Tyler Dawson became best friends when we were kids and during our first semester in this shit hole of a high school we promised ourselves to stick together no matter what. I lifted up my head to see him staring right at me, the best part of Tyler was that he didn't have one ounce of pity on his face; if he did he was pretty damned good at hiding it, what was worse was the memory of him being there at the hospital, and I hoped that he wouldn't mention it.

"Hey Tyler . . . . how's it been?" I didn't really know what to say to him all I wanted to do was lay my head back down, it was different now it used to be so much easier before, but now it was complicated I really didn't know how or what to say to my friends anymore, especially Tyler he saw me at my worse at the hospital.

"I wanted to ask you something." Tyler seemed to be nervous which was really unusual, and I guess it seemed I couldn't avoid any questions.

"Please don't Tyler . . . . I don't want to talk about that day—I'll slap the crap out of you if you ask about it—you're not going to like it very much." I sat up straighter to look tougher.

"No it's not that . . . . it's just I wanted to . . . .

"Ugh . . . . your hesitating to much Tyler would you just come out with it, and ask me the damn question—what do you want do you need help with the chem. test or something, I know your lacking in the studying department."

"No—not that either . . . I just wanted to ask you if you wanted to go to the Autumn Dance with me, you know get your mind off a few things I think it will be good for you." I was floored I had no idea—Dancing+Tyler=who would have thought?

"You want to go to the dance . . . . with me!" I practically jumped out of my chair.

"Hey you two quiet back there. Don't you see we're trying to have class?" I looked up to see Mr. Robert staring at me and Tyler.

"Sorry Mr. Robert." He turned back to the board to continue writing down a formula.

I sat down and put my hand to my face—yup I was embarrassed.

I turned back to stare at Tyler and tried to think of a good response to Tyler's question.

"I think maybe this isn't the best place to talk about this Tyler." I tried to be nice about it.

"Okay ya . . . . we'll talk about it later." the bell rang class was dismissed for lunch I was the first out of my set and out the door—I sat down at our usual table we sat at the same exact place as we did since the beginning of the year nothing really changed—well Me and Tammy Bloom did, but

Tyler didn't he still was as immature now as he was when he was younger, but it was still weird how sometimes he could be serious.

After Tyler's weird ass question, I was off in my own little world thinking about things and oddly enough David, and that really weird ass dream.

"Anne . . . are you listening to me?"

"Hmm . . . what, oh ya I'm listening Tammy."

"Anne are you okay? You're not really being yourself today."

Well, there was a question, how the heck was I going to answer that one.

"I'm okay—it's just been a hard couple of months for me."

Tammy was always so dense, but I couldn't help forgiving her all the time, even if I was in a bad mood.

Heck I knew Tammy Bloom when we were kids as well—At age ten Tammy showed up at my door offering thin mints, and if she sold two more boxes she would get a shiny new bike . . . I giggled at her and told her she looked funny in her green uniform and hat . . . she giggled in return and told me I looked funny in my witch costume I wore all the time and ever since then we were thick as thieves—oh and Tammy got that shiny new bike I made sure of it. I was brought back out of my thoughts again.

"Anne I was wondering . . . if it's not too much to ask . . . do you want to go to the mall with me today—you know to get your mind of a few things." Why the heck did Tammy and Tyler think I needed to clear my mind? I didn't need too I needed to keep thinking about my Mom it was only two damn months since her death—plus I didn't know why everyone was asking me to go anywhere with them—I really didn't feel like going anywhere at all, but I guess I couldn't take it out on her, and I didn't want to disappoint Tammy either, but there was one thing I wouldn't let happen I wouldn't let anything clear my mind of my Mom. I did the most selfless thing I could ever do.

"Ya I'll go to the mall with you Tammy." It had to be done.

"Can I come to?" Tyler mumbled between to bites of his hamburger as he sat right next to me.

"Ugh you're a pig Tyler—speak with your mouth closed! Tammy shook her head in disapproval "I don't know if shopping with two girls is your type of thing Tyler."

"Na I don't mind, just as long as I get to hang out with you Anne, seeing how you don't like to be around pigs Tammy." Tyler took a big bite out of his hamburger, and smiled an evil smile at Tammy God I was hoping that he wouldn't bring up anything about the dance.

"Oh shut up Tyler eat your food—Tammy smiled. "Okay then I'll see you two at nine—at your house Anne."

Ravendell Mall

When I got home I was kind of shocked that I was actually going to do something with my day, even though I was used to the fact of staying in my room, I didn't do much of anything for two months just did my homework and hide in my room—Dad was worried but he tried to understand my method of grieving. Dad would walk pass my doorway and always asked me if I was doing any better, but I would always answer back: 'I would be okay if Mom were here' Dad never really had an answer to that and he would walk away. I was also worried about the whole Tyler thing and dance, nothing ever good came out of a room full of kids and spiked punch.

It was eight thirty and I could hear the doorbell ring while I was getting ready. I really didn't feel like running down the flight of stairs. So I ignored it hoping Dad would get it for me. Sure enough Dad was yelling up at me from the stairs.

"Tyler's here Anne!"

"Okay Dad I'll be down in a minute!" I was dressed in my finest today, skinny Tripp pants with chains and a black t-shirt branded with a crow. I spiked my hair to give it a messy look it was my Mom's favorite look of mine. I let out a puff of air and turned off everything in my room before I went down stairs. There was nothing left to do in my room, so I made the ultimate decision and dragged my ass down stairs. I got to the last step Tyler was standing right next to the post of the stairs.

"Hey Anne." Tyler was looking like his usual self, He had on a long sleeved skull animal t-shirt and black pants with crazy ass steel toed boots, and his black hair was in a messy sort of style, but in a good way.

"How are you holding up today?" Tyler had that look on his face I knew this was going to happen he basically carried me out of my Mom's room. I could feel my heartache at that very moment.

"I just don't know Tyler—it's hard for me right now—and with you it's just hard to . . . . I don't know." I made a break for it and went to the living room to find my boots propped up against the sofa.

"I did what I had to do Anne—whenever you want to talk about it—you know I'm here for you just remember that Anne."

"Thanks I'll keep that in mind Tyler." I wasn't ready at all.

When nine o'clock rolled around I was ready to go, Tyler seemed like he had a lot on his mind, but he kept it to himself. Tyler and I headed out the front door and watched as Tammy drove up the street. Tammy pulled up next to Tyler's car she had the windows rolled down music blasting, but I couldn't really tell what kind of bubble gum pop she was playing this time.

Tyler leaned into the passenger side window, smiling his evil grin he saved only for Tammy.

"So I see your still listening to that trash disguised as so called music." Tyler laughed and opened the door for me. I closed the door behind me expecting Tyler to jump into his car.

"Oh no Tyler your coming with us—no chance you're driving that bucket of bolts behind me I will not be seen with that car Tyler." I couldn't believe Tammy said that—those were grounds for a punch in the face. I didn't know what he was going to say, but knowing Tyler whatever he was going to say was going to sting like hell—Tyler looked at his car and then back at Tammy.

"I have you know Tammy that my car has more class then you." That damn smile slide across his face again. I shrunk back into the passenger seat and put my face into my hands.

"Ugh I really do hate you Tyler." I took a glance at Tammy she was pouting alright—she wasn't even looking at Tyler anymore she was just glaring at his car. I looked at Tyler he was still leaning on the passenger door.

"Just get in the car Tyler." I didn't understand why Tyler and Tammy always fought each other it was frustrating as hell.

It was like that when they were kids too—always kicking and screaming at one another and me always being in the middle of the endless war.

"Alright anything for little miss princess Anne." Tyler pushed himself off the passenger door and climbed into the back seat. I could hear Tammy give off a little frustrated sigh.

"Just ignore it Tammy you know Tyler just does this for kicks." I was doing my best to get her to move her car.

"Ya whatever Tyler's such a jerk." Tammy angrily grabbed the steering wheel and finally pulled out my drive way.

The rest of the time Tammy didn't bother having a conversation with me. I shrugged it off and kept myself busy looking out the window.

It took us awhile to get to the mall Tyler was sitting in the back jamming to his music, you could hear the heavy electric guitar and slamming drums coming from his ear phones it was a wonder how he wasn't completely deaf by now. Tammy pulled me out of my thoughts by finally asking a question I wish she hadn't.

"So Anne have you thought about going to the Autumn Dance yet, because I really think it will be a lot of fun for you." She sounded so hopeful—I seriously didn't want to go, and on top of that I didn't want to tell her that Tyler asked me to go with him. I started moving around nervously in the passenger seat I wish I had sat in the back.

It took an hour to get to the mall, but we finally made it to Ravendell mall without another awkward conversation.

Tammy practically flew to the doors of the mall and was giggling hysterically when she rammed into them.

"Honestly Anne—how did you become friends with Tammy?" Tyler whispered my way.

"Because I got used to Tammy as we grew up—so get over it." I jabbed Tyler in the chest.

"Hey alright I give, you know you don't have to stab me in the chest every time I say something stupid—you have crazy freakin long nails that cause damage to my chest Anne." Tyler was rubbing the spot I got him; it made me smile to cause Tyler a little pain.

"Hey theirs that smile I haven't seen that in a while."

"Ugh Tyler I don't think Anne needs to hear your crap right now—Let's see what we're going to do . . . I know what I'm going to do!"

"What? Going to Abercrombie and bitch again?" Tyler was rolling once he got that insult out.

"Ha ha very funny Tyler your such a fucking idiot at least my clothes look fashionable and not something that was grabbed out of the nearest Dumpster R US." Tyler didn't hesitate one bit.

"Bitch!"

"Jerk!

This continues routine was getting on my damned nerves. "You two really need to get over yourselves . . . Tammy where the heck are we going?!"

Finc I'll let it go . . . . Well I'm going to look at some dresses; my Mom works at the bridal shop theirs some really nice dresses there. I've had my eye on this really cool red dress; I'm totally getting a great discount!"

Most times I really didn't get Tammy, it's like she talked in a different language; maybe its Barbie doll language or something—I've never really understood.

"Well you know where Tyler and I are going to be, just meet us there after you're done."

"Oh come on Anne you're always go to that book store, why don't you just ditch blimp head and come with me . . . . maybe we can find you a dress for the dance."

"Hey I'm standing right here you know!" Tyler was giving Tammy the death stare.

"Don't start you two I'll go, but I want to go the book store first, I've been needing something to read."

"Ya me to . . . something with action!" Tyler said while throwing up his fist.

"My my my—I'm surprised." Tammy had a huge smile on her face.

"About what?" Tyler asked with a glare on his face.

"That you can read!" She was giggling way before she even had the snide remark out.

"Okay . . . okay you two need to break it up. Let's just go to the book store already."

"Oh Tyler knows I just say those things out of love." Tammy couldn't get past her laughter as we walked toward the entrance of the bookstore.

"And you know Tammy I say those things out of hate." Tammy was sticking her tongue out at Tyler, some people saw her they couldn't help, but laugh at her. What the hell are you staring at you dumb shits!" Tyler could be overly defensive when it came to me and Tammy which didn't make sense, because Tammy and Tyler would always fight.

"Calm down Tyler! Let's just go look for some books." The people were already halfway ahead of us do to the fact that Tyler scared the crap out of them.

"Fine!"

"Alright, five minutes that's all you two get, I really want that dress."

Tammy was never a reader like me and Tyler were, but I knew she would do anything to make me go shop with her.

God I never knew a person who loved shopping so much, as I walked into the book store I went to the fiction area and she went to the magazine area.

"At least she reads something." I said with a sigh.

"Ya very smart, flimsy pages with pictures on them, way to go!" Tyler said with utter sarcasm.

"You know Tyler . . . she really does try, but she just can't get into what we get into. Tammy is a good person over all, you should know that by now we've been friends since we were little."

"I know things have changed since we were little Anne and sometimes I just like bugging her; it's just way too easy." Tyler said seriously.

"Oh be quiet and look for some interesting books for me." I stabbed him in the chest for good measure again.

"AHHHH! Alright miss demanding, just as long as I get away from those crazy nails. I'll look on this side for you." Tyler walked to the other side of the aisle as I walked to the other side. I really wanted a good fiction book something that would keep my mind off the real world.

I turned the corner and bumped right into someone, they must have had a lot of books because all of them fell to the floor.

"Oh god . . . I'm sorry." My voice cracked. Gosh I always had to mess up the most simplest of things. All I had to do was look for a book, but I always had to be a clumsy idiot.

"Oh I'm sorry . . . . Anne is that you?"

I felt myself go cold. As carefully as I could I looked up. The first thing I saw was his green eyes.

"Oh . . . um . . . Hi David." My worst nightmare was coming true and at that very moment Tyler was entering that nightmare.

"Hey! I leave you alone for a couple of seconds and you cause destruction!" Crap this was really bad I didn't want to rein act the display that had happened that unfaithful night, and I really didn't want to have an awkward conversation with David and having Tyler present was even worse.

I stood up so fast I felt like I was going to faint right then and there, I took one long breath and recovered, I didn't know what to do with my hands so I just shoved them into my pockets.

"Take it easy Anne it looks like you're going to freakin throw up." Tyler had a smile on his face as he walked up beside me.

"Shut up Tyler, not right now." I tried whispering that to him, but I could tell David noticed.

"Okay Fine—hey man let me get those for you."

"Tyler was already down on one knee picking some of the books up."

"Don't worry about it . . . . Tyler was in the process of handing David some of the books. "Don't recognize me Tyler?" Oh god here it comes—I was in shock glued to the spot I was standing in.

Tyler looked at David . . . . I mean it was only two months that had passed, but the realization of who David was dawned on Tyler.

"Oh ya David . . . . ya I remember you." I could tell Tyler's feelings were taking a turn for the worse. "Here these are yours" Tyler shoved the books into David's chest it didn't even seem to faze David much. David turned his full attention on to me.

"So how have you been Anne?" I looked at Tyler he had his arms crossed over his chest and seemed to be fuming a bit, but he kept his cool. I looked back at David.

"I've been doing okay . . . I just . . . ."

"Anne! Tyler! Where are you guys? Your five minutes are up!"

I felt my stomach jerk; I couldn't believe it I never once mentioned my Moms Doctor to Tammy.

"There you are . . ." I felt like I was going to have a panic attack, I couldn't say anything, it was like my voice was taken away from me.

"Um . . . Anne are you okay?" Tammy walked up to me with concern on her face

With every fiber of my power I could steer up I found my voice.

"Yes . . . I'm fine Tammy . . . She was staring at me and Tyler and then realized that there was someone else in our group.

"Oh hi! Tammy tended to be overly excited when she met new people it was a little weird. Well Anne aren't you going to introduce me to your friend?"

"Oh . . . um this is David . . . David this is Tammy."

"Hi".

They shook each others hands and smiled a brief smile. Tyler bumped into the introduction "This is her Mom's Ex Doctor . . . Tammy." Tammy's smile went away as quick as it went on. "Oh um . . . I didn't . . ." I bumped in to cut off the tension that was starting to form.

"It's fine Tammy."

I saw that some of David's books were still on the floor; I bent down to gather them up.

"That's okay Anne . . . I'll get them."

David bent down and we both met eye to eye, I couldn't look away.

I stood up so fast, but this time I lost my footing.

"Hey . . . watch it."

David grabbed me, we were so close I could smell him, oddly enough he smelled sweet. All of a sudden some sort of vision formed. There was a man his face was faded out but I could tell he was happy he was holding something in his hand it looked like a black rose. Again with the old fashioned clothing I knew this couldn't have been right to have in my head. The vision faded and I was back in the book store.

"Seriously Anne what's with you?" Tyler looked a little upset.

"I'm fine I just stood up to fast . . . um . . . we have to go, it was nice seeing you again David.

"Um . . . ya . . . it was nice seeing you again to Anne."

I grabbed Tammy by her arm and I headed out of the book store as fast as my legs would allow me. I turned around to see Tyler backing away from David he seemed to be looking at him in a way that disgusted him. David was gathering his books and shaking his head—if he were saying something I wouldn't have been able to hear any of it. I shook my head and focused on getting myself out of there. "Hey Anne you never told me that you're Moms Doctor was freakin handsome!"

"Ya well Tammy it didn't seem important to mention at the time now just leave it be, I don't always have to tell you everything Tammy."

"Ya well I want to know your thoughts on this really hot Doctor!"

"Look, I don't want to talk about David right now, I'll talk about it when I'm good and ready." I had her by the arm still we finally made it out the book store. Tammy yanked her arm out of my hand. I stopped to look at her a smile was slowly growing on her face.

"What Tammy?

"You like him Anne I can tell!" she crossed her arms over her chest.

"Shut up Tammy!"

Confession

"I don't like him Tammy." I was breathing rather heavily and I started to feel a slight headache coming my way.

"Yes you do Anne I wasn't born yesterday and I'm not stupid!" I was walking pass stores and not really paying any attention to where I was going, Tammy was keeping up with my stride.

"Wait up you guys—you're walking to fast!" Tyler was still behind us when we left the book store.

"Then pick up those girly legs of yours and catch up! Honestly I don't know how you got through high school without getting your ass kicked by the football team." Tyler eventually caught up to my side.

"The football team was way to busy to kick my ass." I knew where this was going.

"Oh really busy with what?" Tammy crossed her arms across her chest.

"Making out with you!" Tyler was laughing and pumping the air with his fist. "Ya! Take that one!"

"Shut up! Tyler I am so going to get you back for that one!"

"You guys please stop fighting!" My head was practically begging for some relief.

"I'm just warning him Anne, he may have gotten me today, but oh I will get him, it may not be today or it may not be tomorrow, but I will get him." She was smiling and batting her eyelashes at Tyler.

"All right . . . fine, just as long as you two get a room, so that way I don't have to hear any of it." The food court was right next to me when I stopped walking.

"Wow that was harsh Anne and what makes you think I want to be in the same room with Tammy at any point of my life."

"Oh just be quiet! I'm going to get something to drink, why don't you two sort out your issues while I'm gone."

I walked up to the nearest place to get a drink; I couldn't think of any reason to continue this whole 'fun eventful day' I really thought I could get over a few things, but my friends just made it worse for me. I paid for my drink and sat down it felt nice just to be sitting their ignoring both of them was the best thing I needed right now. Closing my eyes and just letting myself calm down for a while seemed to work, but I could only do that for so long. I could feel the table move it was a sign that someone was sitting down.

"So Anne aren't you going to spill anything about the guy you just introduced me too."

I let my head fall to the table and kept it their while I mustered up what little strength I had left to talk to Tammy.

"Ugh . . . . why?"

"Because he's cute, and I'm nosy in case you haven't noticed." I gave a halfhearted laugh and lifted up my head to look at Tammy.

"Oh I've noticed that about you Tammy, but I really don't want to talk about David."

"Pretty pleaaaaaaaseeeeeeeee with sugar on top!" Tammy was a type of person who didn't know anything about boundaries.

"Fine if I tell you about him, will you promise to keep the fighting down to a minimum with Tyler?" I couldn't believe I was going to tell her all my deepest and darkest secrets.

"By the way—where is Tyler?"

"Tyler's stuffing his face with as much food as possible." Tammy smiled. Okay okay so forget about Tyler and let's talk about you and David."

"Well . . . . David . . . I hesitated for a moment I wasn't too sure if this was a good idea.

"Come on girl spit it out I'm getting anxious over here!" Tammy was practically lying across the table to listen to what I had to say.

"Well David was my Mom's Doctor." I could feel myself blushing.

"I know that part already! Get to the point Anne!"

"Alright god!" This was making it so much worse for me.

"Sorry Anne I'm just excited."

"Okay." I shook my head.

"So what's going on between you two? I sense a lot of tension between you guys."

"It's not that . . . Tammy I think I might have feelings for him." I slumped down in my seat and groaned. I had no idea what I was going to do with myself.

"I wasn't born yesterday Anne . . . . I saw that a mile away."

This was Tammy's reaction to my confession, well I tried hiding it, but there really wasn't any way to keep anything from Tammy . . . if someone has one ounce of feelings for someone she could track it out like a blood hound.

"Ya well I know you weren't Tammy—it's just I didn't want to believe in these feelings I figured they would go away as time went on—but they haven't—it's like ever since my Mom died we just kept on bumping into each other."

"It was enough seeing him at the funeral; I can't keep my head clear when David's near me."

I knew very well I couldn't tell her about the strange dreams or visions whatever the heck they were.

"Okay . . . let's think for a minute."

That was a laugh Tammy having an honest to god thought was really hard to believe—I always thought Tammy had something way better to do then to actually have the time to think something through.

"Look Tammy I don't need any of your crazy ideas. I thought I could change things by going out and having fun . . . . but I don't think it's a good idea for me right now. I just need to be alone for a while." The look on her face was of complete outrage, but the idea of staying home and not risking seeing David again would make things a lot easier for me.

"Anne don't do this . . . you really need to be around friends . . . you can't always be alone even though you think it's the right thing . . . . please don't do anything you might regret in the long run . . . . there is no reason for you to be alone."

There were many things running through my mind as Tammy was saying all of this, I wanted to tell Tammy that this was how it was supposed to be, but I held back. My Dad was the best excuse to use I couldn't tell her that I wanted to avoid David cause I knew the next thing she would say is 'you're running away from your feelings.' "I have my Dad it's not like I'll be alone . . . .

"Yes I know but it's not good enough . . . it seems your Dad is avoiding you and your Moms death . . . it's not right and you know it . . . . why can't you see that Anne, it's not healthy for you."

"Look Oprah if I wanted advice I would ask, but I don't need you telling me what I need and what I don't need, I feel that I need to be alone, and that's my final choice.

My Dad's fine, he just needs to catch up on his work, my Dad just doesn't have the time to sit down and talk to me—his boss doesn't give him a break . . . that's all."

"Anne . . . please don't push me away . . . I'm your best friend and believe it or not Tyler really has some real feelings for you and for as long as I can remember we've never really split apart, I know that me and Tyler don't see things eye to eye, but give us a chance to help you through this . . . that's all I ask of you." Boy I couldn't believe Tammy was trying this hard to keep me from doing something I might regret, but I still felt the same way.

"Tammy just understand . . . I need to be alone . . . . I need to clear my mind out . . . . maybe even go away for a while."

"Why would you want to go away, why can't you just stay here with me and Tyler, why can't you just let us in—please don't run away from the people who really care about you."

At that moment I was pretty much speechless, which was shocking because I was never at a loss for words. I never knew Tammy had it in her to say things that were so meaningful, I didn't think I could have come up with half the things that were coming out of her mouth, but I guess I shouldn't have been too shocked she was my best friend.

"I have to go; I just need to go home Tammy."

For the first time in a long time I walked away from Tammy, which was the hardest thing I had ever done in my whole entire life, but I knew it had to be done. I could hear Tammy calling for me, but I lost myself in the crowds of the mall.

Realization

As I ran out of the mall I realized I didn't have a ride, but I couldn't turn back now. Things were said that couldn't be fixed at the moment. I knew I had to see Tammy at school, but it was better for me to not be foolish. So the next best thing was to hitch a ride on a bus, which by all means would not be comfortable, but I had to deal with it. I dug through my stuff and found a couple of dollars which was enough for bus fair, as I closed my bag it started raining which of course was my luck, but it really didn't matter, it was a long walk to find where the bus stop was, but I made it to my destination. I waited for bus 70 to show its iron face and an hour and soaked clothes later eventually it did, I boarded the bus and sat down all the way in the back. It was getting really late and I wondered if Dad was getting worried—my phone hadn't gone off at all. I looked out the window to see the water streaming at an angle as bus 70 speed past buildings and parked cars, I liked seeing the faces of people being obscured it was like art, this was the only time people looked like one another I guess it really didn't matter if they were beautiful or not.

Bus 70 rushed passed unknown areas of Ravendell, Seattle and I realized that I hardly knew anything about where I lived other then it rained to damn much here. I never took the time to actually see what was around me. The only thing I knew was home and that was it, I didn't know what would come after high school, what my life would be like, I didn't have a Mom to confide in about those things, I took advantage of my Mom at the beginning, but when I was losing her to cancer I tried everything to ease my guilt, and nothing ever did. Even now that she was gone I could never forgive myself.

The bus halted at its final stop. I jumped out of my set and walked out of the bus as fast as I could. I knew my house was a few blocks from the bus stop, but it felt like forever to walk such a short distance with the rain and all. There was a chill in the air which made me feel so much colder. I walked the rest of the way and found that all the lights were on in the house, and a very expensive looking black car parked out in front of the house. I knew this couldn't be good.

Tyler's car was still parked on the side of the drive way—I guess Tammy and Tyler were having it out in the mall about me.

If someone was there it was a distraction for my Dad to not yell at me—there was only one way to find out what the final verdict was of this horrible day. What I thought was a long walk to the house felt longer to get to the front door. I grabbed the keys out of my bag and unlocked the door. All I wanted was to go to my room and sleep and never think about this day ever again, but I knew I wasn't going to make it to my room. As I opened the front door the atmosphere of the house was very different; I couldn't put my finger on it. I could hear voices coming from the living room, one voice sounded oddly familiar. I began to get very worried and frightened at the same time. I heard my Dad's voice it sounded like he said "that must be her right now". Of course that was never good, there was a conversation going on about me, I didn't know what I was going to happen.

"Anne is that you." I couldn't tell if Dad was stressed or crazy. I don't even know why Dad even asked that question anymore, because we were the only two left living in this death trap of a house, but today I would give him the benefit of the doubt.

"Ya . . . Dad it's me?" I was even more worried to walk into the living room, but as slowly as possible—I pushed myself to do it, yup you guessed it I found myself to be in shock, and glued to the very spot I was standing in yet again. "Guess who's just dropped by to see us." All I could do was cough to try to get back my bearings, but it was so hard to, David was just staring at me, I didn't understand why he had to do that. Obviously he was the one to start off the conversation.

"Hey Anne? I just thought I'd stop by to see if you were okay. You seemed troubled." My thoughts were racing and I couldn't even breathe right. They probably thought I was going nuts or something.

"I . . . um . . . I'm fine." I couldn't believe David was here in our house. Dad seemed to be back to normal Dad just wondered through the house like a zombie until he had to go to work, it was weird Dad seemed to be happy for once.

"David told me you guys bumped into each other at the mall today."

Well that was a bit of an understatement (I ran into him literally). "Well ya . . . we did Dad."

"That's good . . . . it seems we need a little bit of excitement around here . . . These past few months haven't been that easy for me and Anne—Anyway kiddo given any thought as to whom you want to go to the Autumn dance with . . . it's right around the corner."

One thing was for certain I didn't want to think about that, and the fact that Tyler wanted me to be his date was off settling.

"Hold on one second Dad I don't think this is the time to have this discussion." David looked like he was very interested in the conversation.

"I'm sorry Dad, but I need to be excused I'm not feeling so well." I walked away and ran to the bathroom. "She' does that a lot doesn't she?" That was the last thing I heard David say before I slammed the door to the hallway bathroom. My bag dropped to the floor providing everyone to hear a loud thud hopefully that didn't bother anyone—I caught myself on the ledge of the sink the reflection of myself in the mirror had changed throughout the years. I knew I was different ever since I was little, every kid made fun of me, because I liked the strange things of life you know not what was normal for a young little girl to like. I couldn't help that my choice of doll was Dracula and not the stupid Barbie doll.

But what I could tell was that I was still a little wet from the rain. My eyeliner was a little smeared but not to the point where it would look horrible. I looked really pale like I was going to be hit by a very bad strain of flu. I took in a couple of deep breaths to clear my head splashed water in my face—it really didn't help. I dried my face and looked up to see myself for one last time I still looked pale. My clothes were a mess but at the moment I just didn't care. With as much courage as I had I switched the bathroom light off and opened the door.

"Are you okay?" I looked up to find David leaning against the hall way wall.

"Oh! . . . . um . . . . David you scared me." It wasn't natural for David to be around as much as he was.

"I'm sorry . . . I didn't mean to scare you Anne."

"David why are you here?" David seemed to be searching for an answer which wasn't there, or so I thought.

"I just wanted to make sure you were okay Anne."

"Look David I'm fine . . . you don't need to check up on me . . . I'm not one of your patients."

Clearly David was concerned, because he wouldn't leave with that.

"I know that . . . but there seems to be something in me that keeps bringing me back too you Anne."

"David I don't know what you're talking about, but I think maybe you should rethink something's—you're a doctor and you shouldn't get emotionally involved with the patient or the patient's family." I didn't want to come across as a cold hearted jerk but this was getting ridiculous.

"I don't get involved with patients, but this is different in so many ways, all I want you to do is trust me . . . . and I know you feel the same way—I saw it in your eyes in the hospital and at the funeral and even now . . . Don't try to deny it cause I know it would be a lie."

Holy crap David knew . . . . I needed to do something.

"Hey! Where do you come off . . . you're acting crazy David . . . .

I wanted throw David off the trail . . . I couldn't tell him a thing—I was distracted by Dads pager buzzing loudly. I heard my Dad coming toward the hallway. "David this isn't right."

I took my chances and went to the hallway table and grabbed my Dad's pager, really anything to get away from David's gaze.

"Hey Dad! Your boss is calling . . . where were you just then?"

"Thanks Anne I probably have to do some more paper work . . . oh I was checking the mail." I could feel David's gaze on the back of my neck, it puzzled me I didn't know what he wanted from me.

"Mr. Black I have to get going it was nice seeing you and your daughter again."

He walked right pass me and took my Dad's hand in a rough hand shake.

"Oh no problem come again anytime. You have meant a lot to this family . . . I have a lot of respect for you David."

"Ya well I wish Anne felt the same way." He looked right at me. David's piercing green eyes got to me again he knew very well what he was doing. Something flashed before my eyes, a vision—a man screaming something, but I couldn't make it out he sounded so heartbroken he was being held back by someone, the scene was over it was just a blur something I just couldn't understand. I shook my head and gained my bearings back. I watched David as he walked right out of our front door, and suddenly the atmosphere began to feel like it was supposed to feel, which was oddly strange.

"Ok . . . . now that company is gone I need to go to work . . . why don't you take an early nap you look out of it." I couldn't believe Dad wasn't angry at me for being late.

"Okay then Dad I guess I'll see you later." Dad walked right out the front door slamming it right behind him. It felt so empty in this great big house it used to smell like roses when they first blossomed, Mom always had the house smelling like a big huge flower, but now it didn't smell like anything Mom left the house completely I couldn't feel her anymore. This frightened me more than anything in the world.

I found myself in my room the only place I knew so well. My stuff was everywhere I just couldn't bring myself to clean it up.

Mom would have already told me to clean my room right about now. I would always hear her coming up the stairway always sighing to herself every time she passed my doorway, no matter what I could always read into those sighs, I'd always shout "I'll clean my room when I can," she would always reply back.

"You're in your room now . . . looks like you have time my dear Anne." But now there would be no sighing anymore and there wouldn't be arguing about it anymore. Tears started to weld up in my eyes. I tried blinking them away, but it was useless, so I just laid down on my bed and cried. I felt like smothering myself with my pillow, and ending my existence right then and there.

David wasn't helping this situation at all—I didn't know what he knew or why he wanted to keep me in his life—I would have to think about that later my head began to ache. I closed my eyes . . . .

But a tapping on my window made my eye's snap open. I looked up at my bedroom window and saw Tyler staring back at me. Tyler didn't look like he was happy I tried wiping away the evidence from my face. I was hesitant at first, but I walked up to my window and opened it for him.

"Stop trying to hide it Anne I'm not stupid." Tyler ducked his way through my window and was standing tall in my room. I cleared my throat and sat down on my bed.

"What do you mean . . . I'm not hiding anything?"

"Come on Anne when are you going to stop treating me like an idiot! You were crying, and don't you dare tell me you weren't!"

"Fine! I was crying. What are you going to do about it?"

"Apparently nothing because you won't let me in, and I'm pretty much getting sick of it Anne."

"Well what do you want from me Tyler—this is really hard for me."

"It's hard for me to see my best friend being eaten inside and out with so much pain."

Boy he really did know how to treat a girl when she felt like crap already.

"And what the hell happened at the mall today Anne? I turned my back for a couple of seconds, and poof your gone—nowhere to be seen. And this guy David—I can't say I really like him all too much." I didn't know where all this was coming from.

"What do you care Tyler?!"

"I care plenty Anne; you just have to let me." Tyler took his place right in front of me sitting down on the floor and crossing his legs.

"So I need you to explain what happened today Anne."

"Why is it so important for you to know?"

"Because I would like to know if the girl I'm taking to the dance is going to be sticking around—that she won't bail out on me at the end of the day."

"Ugh . . . Tyler you just won't let up on that will you?"

"No not until you say yes, and not until you explain to me what is going on with you." I wanted to slap the crap out of him, but I couldn't bring myself to do it.

"What if I don't want to explain anything to you? What if I just want to crawl into a hole and disappear forever?"

"Well you better believe that I will follow you wherever you go." That bothered the crap out of me when he said that.

"And if you don't want to explain anything to me about today—expect me to crawl through that window every single day."

"I'll lock the window Tyler."

"You know you won't ever lock me out Anne."

"Ugh I know . . . . How was Tammy when I left?" Tyler didn't seem to want to change the subject, but he slumped his shoulders and gave in.

"Man if there were ever a day I could get you back for that; I would. Tammy was completely hysterical!"

"I'm sorry Tyler." I got up and went to my dresser. There was a picture of us when we were younger. Tammy and I were smiling, but Tyler was always Tyler making his crazy ass faces. I grabbed the picture frame and held it up to get a better look. I could hear Tyler get up from the floor. I looked up in my dresser mirror Tyler was looking over my shoulder he had a serious look on his face.

"Man that was a long time ago; a couple of misfits weren't we?" I can't believe you still have this." Tyler grabbed it out of my hands and sat down at the edge of my bed.

"Of course I do why wouldn't I?"

"Look at my face. Looks like someone hit the shit out of it!" He was laughing and running his hand through his hair. "Man those were the days . . . . a small smile appeared on his face but slowly turned into a slight frown.

"I didn't mean for anything to change Tyler, they just did . . . . and I'm really sorry for that."

"Why are you apologizing? You didn't kill your Mom." Tyler set the photo down on the nightstand next to my bed. He sighed and got up from my bed.

"You know Anne . . . . I'm always going to be here for you." Tyler walked up to me closing the nice comfortable space that was between us. I cleared my throat and backed up a few paces.

"I know I've always known that, and I'm thankful for that Tyler." It was getting dark outside I hadn't turned on a light in my room which made this situation even worse.

"What are we at some thanksgiving dinner? Seriously Anne you got to come up with something way better than that." Changing the subject felt like a good idea again.

"It's getting late—you should probably go home now." Tyler lowered his head and let out a sigh.

"No I won't go."

"Why?"

"Because I'm getting this really bad feeling that I won't be seeing you again . . . . and I think David will have something to do with it . . . I saw how he was looking at you in the book store—fucking pissed me off."

"Why did you have to bring up David?" Tyler walked away from me and sat down in a chair that was in the corner of my room.

"Because I feel like the two of you have feelings for each other." Had to hand it to Tyler he wasn't blind towards it either.

"Do you know how stupid you're sounding right now Tyler!?" I crossed my arms over my chest.

"No I don't Anne! But I know I'm right weather you like it or not."

"Well there's nothing going on, if that makes you feel any better Tyler."

"I don't know what to feel right now Anne, but I'm willing to keep you away from that sort of trouble."

"What makes you think David is trouble?! David is a freakin Doctor Tyler for crying out loud, what's he going to do, stab me to death with a scalpel?"

I turned around to look at Tyler he was staring at me as if I were hiding something, and he would do anything to find out what that was.

"Looks can be very deceiving Anne, trust me I know when I see trouble." I walked to one of my lamps and switched it on, it was getting way to dark in my room and I was beginning to feel very anxious.

"Fine I'll be careful." I turned away from my lamp and placed my hands in my pockets.

"Promise me." Tyler got up from my chair and stood in front of my window.

"Ugh I promise Tyler." Tyler looked at me for a while.

"Wish I could believe you Anne."

"Is that all you needed to know Tyler?"

"No not really, but I guess I'm going to have to leave with what I got, but soon you have to tell me what's going on in that mind of yours."

"Ya sure—but I really don't think you want to know, it's pretty messed up."

"Look at me Anne, I practically live for messed up shit, you can tell me anything and I won't cringe or make you feel like an idiot for thinking it was messed up in the first place. Let's just say I have a whole other side of me that you've never really seen. You're just going to have to give me a chance to show you that side."

"I . . . ."

"No don't say anything, not until you think things over. Not until you have a better answer for me. And not until you realize that the friends you have are all you got."

Tyler turned away from me and walked onto my roof. Tyler leaned into my window again before he made his dramatic exit.

"I hope I'll be seeing you Anne."

Saturday

Saturday morning I woke up groggy with the worst head ach ever—the conversation I had with Tyler weighed heavy on my mind—I looked out the window—the rain outside was getting worse there was a clap of thunder off in the distance. I wondered if Dad made it home okay—my thoughts were all mixed up and all I wanted to do was go back to sleep, my eyes felt puffy I couldn't help crying after Tyler left. I couldn't hold back anymore not even one tear stayed in my system. The bed covers were all twisted around my legs it made me feel uncomfortable I felt so trapped and useless, and unprepared for the day. Questions would be asked if I stayed in bed all day I didn't want Dad to become worried about me, but maybe he wouldn't. Dad never had time for most things let alone worrying about me. I finally untwisted the blankets from my legs, and I reluctantly placed my feet on the wood floor the coldness of the floor sent chills up my legs—I ignored it the best I could. The clothes I had on yesterday were wrinkled as hell; I usually tried not to sleep in my clothes, but I had to admit yesterday was hell.

I could hear noises coming from downstairs. I felt way too tired to change into a big shirt—I shook my head and walked to my closet door—I was about to open it when my bed room door was thrown opened and Tammy ran in uninvited as usual.

"I took the liberty of coming over, you're Dad looks really tired . . . and you don't look so hot yourself." Well that clued me in that Dad was home.

Tammy looked a little angry and annoyed at the same time.

"I can't believe you left me at the mall like that Anne!"

"Well thanks for the complement that was just what I needed, and stop yelling I have a headache."

"That's not what I meant and you know it, and I can yell whenever I want to!"

"Okay drama queen, so what do you want?" This could be interesting.

"What I want is for you to be the way you were before your Mom's death."

I couldn't think why Tammy was being so selfish . . . if Tammy were in my shoes I don't think she would find me being such a jerk. Oh and I don't think she would ever find herself in my combat boots . . . . I know that for sure.

"You're my best friend Tammy . . . . I thought you would be more understanding. How could you ask me that, it's ridiculous!"

"I am your friend . . . it's just . . . you don't have to be this way, all depressing and crap—you know."

I wanted to slap the crap out of Tammy for talking out of her ass, but in this case I couldn't bring myself to ever hit my best friend, but I did feel like striking something right about now.

Look Tammy don't be this way—it really sucks. I'm going back to bed I would rather sleep then listen to this."

Huh . . . Ya—but what was the off chance that Tammy would ever leave, I guess it would be slim to none.

"Well . . . sleeping away your problems is not a good way to solve them Anne."

"What! . . . this isn't a "simple problem!" I lost my Mom . . . you will never understand that Tammy you have your Mom . . . until you lose her then you can come talk to me Tammy."

"Okay . . . maybe I won't understand now, but that doesn't give you the right to act like the biggest jerk on the face of the planet . . . Yes your Mom is gone I got that . . . but eventually you're going to have to get over it."

"It's been a couple of months, are you nuts Tammy!"

She had to be kidding me. I mean I couldn't believe Tammy thought she could come in here and act as if she could "fix me" this was to overwhelming.

"No I'm not nuts . . . maybe I don't know!" I couldn't believe this.

"Tammy I would like you to do me a favor . . . .

"What would that be Anne?"

"I would like for you to leave." That was probably something Tammy wasn't expecting because the look on her face was of complete shock it seemed like she wasn't too sure what to do. Tammy turned a little.

"No I'm not leaving—there's no way I'm going to leave this room until you get yourself together Anne."

I couldn't believe it. Tammy was trying to boss me around in my own room, not to mention this wasn't even her house. It was like she was forgetting her place.

"Fine . . . . I'll go." I grabbed my boots my bag and my car keys and made a break for it. I slipped right pass Tammy and took the stairs by two (of course trying to keep myself from falling). In no time I was at the bottom of the stairway shoving my feet into my boots. I looked up to see my Dad standing in front of me. (Dad did look tried) he's hair was graying he used to have really black hair and gray eye's that had life, but now he just looked so sad and incomplete.

"Where are you going in such a hurry—and aren't those the clothes you wore yesterday?"

To be honest Dad began to look pretty worried which almost made me cry I wanted to tell him everything I was feeling, but I couldn't do it.

"I have to go."

"Go where Anne . . . why don't you just talk to me?" well the offer was tempting but I just couldn't came out with it.

"I just need to think for a while I'll be back later Dad."

I got up from the stairs and headed for the door.

"This can't go on forever Anne sooner or later—we will talk weather you like it or not, I know it doesn't seem like I want to talk, but I think it's time. I'll let you go this time."

"Gee thanks Dad—it's a date." I heard Tammy coming down the stairs.

"Got to go!" I flung the door open and ran out to my car.

Black Rose

I high tailed it out of the drive way, and out of the neighborhood it took two exits and a really long road—but I finally pulled up to Ravendell cemetery—the small road leading up to the cemetery made me feel nervous. I hadn't set foot in it since Mom's funeral I parked my car to the left of the road and sat there for a while my phone range, but I ignored it. I wasn't too sure if I was ready to do this—but this was the only place I could think of to get away from everyone—I managed to open my car door, and walk to the opening of the cemetery. I took in a breath and gave myself a push the rain began to pick up with each step I took—to bad I didn't think of bringing my umbrella.

I knew where my Mom was she was exactly right in the heart of the cemetery—rain seeped through my shirt causing my teeth to chatter I realized I didn't have flowers my heart sank some daughter I was. Mom's tomb stone was a couple of paces away my heart began to race.

"I'm sorry Mom." Tears began to run down my face.

The rain had drenched everything I was wearing, but I really didn't care. There was grass growing all over my Mom's tomb stone. I mean I didn't know what it took for people to get off their butts for lack of a better word and keep this place semi-nice. I pulled at the grass and my frustrations took over I wanted the grass to be gone—I didn't want it touching my Mom's tomb—I ripped at the grass falling to my knees as I did this I kept tearing and yanking—mud began to splatter all over me, but I didn't care I wanted to see my Mom's name.

"What are you doing Anne?" I nearly jumped out of my skin. I turned around to find David leaning on one of the dead trees.

"David you startled me . . . what are you doing here?" I came to realize that I must have looked crazy ripping at the grass and crying—I looked at my hands they were red and splattered with mud . . . I was completely soaked . . . I glanced back up at David.

David looked different not like his usual self yesterday he was dressed casually something a Doctor would wear—This time David was dressed in dark blue jeans scuffed up boots a black t-shirt and a black leather jacket his black hair styled in a messy look and when I looked into his dark green eyes my legs shook a little

"Happened to be passing through Anne."

I began to shiver again and I felt a little dizzy. The rain was still getting worse.

"You okay Anne?" David pushed himself off the dead tree and closed the space in between us.

"I'm fine . . . It's just a little cold . . . I really wasn't thinking David."

"I can see that Anne."

I looked back at my Mom's tomb stone I hadn't really done much good I made more of a mess.

"I just wanted to see my Mom David."

"Here take my jacket Anne." I really didn't get a chance to say no, but it was nice to not have the rain hit me anymore.

"Thanks David."

"No problem . . . know let's get you home Anne . . ."

"I can't go back there." I backed away from him.

"Why Anne?"

"Because I can't handle being around my Dad anymore and Tyler is beginning to act strange and forget Tammy she's becoming . . . I don't know!" I turned to look at my Mom's resting place. My hands felt ice cold I placed them in the pockets of David's jacket—I felt something soft against my left hand—it felt like petals of a flower I took it out of his pocket and looked at the flower.

"David." I whispered his name softly.

"What is it Anne?" I turned to face David.

"Where did you get this?" David looked at my hand.

"It's just a flower Anne."

"It's not just a flower David it's a black rose . . . I've seen this before." David's face became serious.

"What do you mean you've seen this before Anne?" I realized I had said to much.

"Nothing David . . .

"No Anne explain what you mean." David walked up to me and grabbed me by my shoulders.

"I don't mean anything by it David it's just cold and I'm not thinking straight." I could feel his grip begin to tighten.

David was so close it made me extremely nervous . . . my vision began to blur.

"No . . . that was the last word that left my lips I was pulled into a vision . . . it was dark and I could hear a woman's scream I didn't understand why it was so dark—the vision faded and I was pulled back into the cemetery. I was on the ground David had his arms wrapped around me he was soaked in just as much rain as I was.

"What happened?" David pulled me back up to a standing position.

"You began to scream Anne."

"No that wasn't me David it was a women I couldn't see . . .

"A women . . . .

Again I had said too much I didn't want David to know about my visions it was way to insane for me—and I didn't want to tell him that every time I had one it was because of him. David closed the gap between us again.

"Please talk to me Anne I want to know." David's eyes began to smolder it was as if they were glowing it terrified me.

"I can't explain it to you David."

"Why can't you Anne I know there's something going on and I want to know how it is you know about this flower."

David looked as if he was ready to grab me again.

"David I wish I could explain it to you, but I don't think this is something I should be talking about."

"Don't you get it Anne . . . why are you making this so hard?

"I think I need more time David."

"Anne I'm here for you . . . .

I pushed myself away from him.

"Just leave me alone David! It's better this way!"

"No it's not Anne! Please tell me!"

"No David it's too crazy!"

All the stress I was feeling started to make me feel light headed. My legs began to feel weak. David had me in his arms before I hit the ground.

"You're coming with me Anne . . . .

That was the last thing I heard David say. I unwillingly blacked out.

Blur

I woke up my eyes felt like crap I rubbed the palms of my hands into my eyes to try to get my vision back, it worked a little bit. I realized I was lying on something soft. There was a pillow propped up behind my head. I managed to move slowly to the edge of what seemed to be a massive bed. The room was so dark I ended up knocking my knees against a dresser as I got off the bed. I finally found myself at the bedroom door I opened it slowly and peeked out. The hallway outside was dimly lit. it was quiet and a little creepy I glanced behind me and decided that I need to explore. As I went to the stairs I took a look at myself I knew very well that I wasn't wearing my clothes from earlier I tried shaking my head to clear my thoughts; I would have to figure out what happened later. Right now I was curious to see where I was. Slowly I descended the stairs and ended up in what look like the main hallway. I couldn't take it anymore I finally decided to say something.

"Hello . . . is anyone there?" David walked into the hallway I was in.

"Hey . . . How are you feeling? Come here Anne you need to sit by the fire . . . you look like your shivering again."

I hadn't even noticed I was shivering again. I probably looked pathetic.

"Where am I? I had crossed my arms over my chest and walked with David to the living room.

"This is my place."

David had to be kidding his house looked like it belonged to a movie star.

"Um—what happened to my car?"

"I called one of my friends to drive your car here it's in my garage."

"Who dressed me?" his face looked stern.

I kind of knew what David's answer would be, and I knew if he told me I would freak.

"I . . . uh . . . he hesitated and looked away from me.

"I don't think I want to know David."

"Are you hungry? Do you need something to drink?"

"No thanks . . . . do you live here by yourself David?"

"Yes I do . . . . this is how it's been my whole life."

"Well don't you have family?"

David walked towards the fire place he seemed to be deep in thought.

"I'm sorry I shouldn't have asked you that."

"There are things that I just don't like talking about and my past is one of them."

David had turned around and looked at me the look on his face was something that made my blood go cold this was making me feel way too nervous.

"I think maybe I should get going David . . . ."

"Where are you going to go Anne?"

"I'll figure that out David."

I took my chances and ran for the front door. Why I was running I didn't even know why. But behind me I could hear David calling my name. I managed to open the front door and hurry right out onto the front porch. I hadn't really planed past the running part, but I knew I had to find the garage. The front yard was enormous. I had no shoes and the damned black dress I was wearing was really annoying. I had no idea where my actual clothes were—I snuck my way into the back of the house and found the garage. I made my way to the door in hoping I would be able to open it myself. Bending down I slipped my fingers under the massive garage door. All of a sudden I heard footsteps coming towards me. I whirled around and found myself face to face with a man . . . . something was off about him.

"Who the hell are you?" I didn't have time to rephrase that sentence.

A very sly smile began to form on his face . . . . I had this feeling in my heart that I couldn't trust him.

"Such bad language coming from a beautiful young lady I'm glad to see David has finally brought home a pet. I've been waiting for this for quite some time."

He was tall and his clothes seemed out of date like he popped out of the 18th century—his hair was black and slicked back and his skin seemed very pale—I couldn't get a good feeling from this guy.

This was getting really weird and I was really hoping David would show up. It was a mistake to run out here in the dark.

"Hold on one minute I am no one's 'pet' David was my Mom's Doctor."

I didn't even know why I was talking to this man when I should very well be leaving this place and get the hell out of here.

"I know very well what David does Anne."

The smile had left his face and know there was this scornful look upon it.

"How did you know my name . . . .

I didn't stick around for the answer . . . I ran away. I could hear him coming after me. My bare feet were hurting so bad that I almost wanted to cry.

"David!" I screamed his name so loudly in hoping he would hear me. There were snarling noses coming from behind me. I turned around and that was the biggest mistake I had made all night. I tripped and ended up rolling down a small hill in the back yard. I felt something pop it took all my courage to not yell out in pain. I was face down at the bottom of the hill I felt something grab me.

"You thought you could get away from me didn't you?"

The man's voice was changed somehow; it sounded rougher. I had no choice but to look—The site of him was so awful and animal like. I screamed so loudly. The creature was laughing so much I thought maybe he was going crazy. His face was changed in a way that made him look so evil and his eyes were glowing red.

"Let go of her . . . or I will kill you! I will finish what we started a long time ago Victor!"

I was plopped down onto the ground again, my shoulder was screaming with pain.

"Oh come on David I was just having a little fun."

"You call messing with my life fun!"

"I couldn't help myself she smells so good, I remember that smell. That smell came from your first human. What was her name again?" If I wasn't mistaken it looked like Victor was drooling. Before I knew it David howled in fury and punched Victor in the face.

I couldn't believe it. This was a whole other side of David I never seen before. The looks on each of their faces were field with rage and malice. There were blows being connected but I couldn't tell who was getting the worse of the damage. I was trying to pull myself away from the danger, and I finally found refuge behind a tree and prayed to God to stop this madness. I put my hands over my ears so I couldn't hear the horrible growls that were emitting from one of them. I could only guess it was coming from Victor.

My hands were yanked away from my ears and I nearly screamed.

"It's me Anne!" I opened my eyes and realized that it was David he had a gash on his forehead.

"Oh my God what just happened?! Who was that man?! What was he talking about?!"

I was scared out of my mind. There were so many questions I wanted answers to but I just didn't know where to begin.

"Anne calm down . . . we need to focus on getting you home right now! It's not safe out here for you." There was absolute fear in his eyes. Something was wrong and I didn't know what to do about it.

"I have to make sure you get home safe Anne."

"Are you okay David?!"

"Don't worry about me Anne. There's no time."

The run back to the garage was agonizing. My shoulder was screaming with pain.

"Please stop! We have to stop! My shoulder is killing me!"

David picked me up and carried me the rest of the way. He entered a code into a keypad on the wall of the garage. The door opened automatically. David sat me on a table that was against the wall.

"David it really hurts! Please do something!" I knew I was acting like a baby but I couldn't help it.

"You need to calm down before you start hyperventilating." David grabbed my face in his hands. He looked me straight in the eyes. That calmed me down. "Okay your shoulder is not dislocated it's badly bruised." He grabbed me and we both headed to my car.

"David backed out of the garage and speed as fast as he could. There was no stopping anywhere. We got to my house at midnight. There was no sign of life which was probably for the best, because I didn't feel like explaining anything to anyone right now.

We both got out of my car. David came to my side and helped me to the front door I was expecting Dad to be waiting for me, but darkness was all that met me as I opened the front door.

Here take this its my number in case anything happens call me." David grabbed my hand and placed the paper in my hand . . . . i looked at my hand and closed it.

Get some rest Anne . . . you're going to need it."

"Can I ask you something?" I turned to David so that he could see my face.

"Sure ask away." David stopped in his tracks and looked right at me.

"Who are you?" I really didn't know why I was asking him, but I felt like there was so much more to what happened tonight.

"I think in time we both will figure that out."

I didn't understand what David meant by that, but given to what had happened tonight, I just nodded.

"Goodnight Anne."

"Goodnight David."

I walked inside and closed the door. As fast as I could I ran to the window nearest to the front door I peered out of it. There was no sign of David only shadows I let the curtain fall back in place.

Tonight's events were freaking out my stomach—I wanted to vomit at that very second. I ran up the stairs not turning any of the lights on—I ran into my room and stood there to catch my breath I sat down on my bed and placed my hand on my shoulder it hurt like hell for sure, but I didn't want to think about it, because it would have made tonight's events real.

Intruder

Sleep was one thing that wouldn't come to me my shoulder wouldn't give up on its angry voyage to keep me awake all night. I pulled myself out of bed and down the stairs dragging myself into the living room sitting myself in front of the TV debating whether or not I should turn it on. I knew there couldn't have been anything on at 3:00 in the morning—Dad was working one of his late nights again he never worked so many hours before Mom died; we were a happy family at one point, but all Dad wanted to do was work late hours and try to avoid the fact that Mom was gone. I knew Dads boss didn't care at all and I didn't understand why the man could be so heartless. What also pissed me off the most was that his co-workers didn't give a crap, ya sure a pat on the shoulder here and there, but nothing really. That place didn't give a shit about my Dad.

A noise outside distracted me from my thoughts. I froze not knowing who would be outside at this hour. There was a creaking of a board on the porch that only meant that someone was intruding our space. I ran to the lamp as quietly as possible and turned it off I was hoping whoever was out there didn't notice. I tried to tell myself that it was nothing that it was all in my head and all I needed to do was to calm down. But when I heard more creaking and clunking of footsteps I knew it wasn't in my head.

Tyler wouldn't be crazy enough to be out this late the risk of getting caught was way too great. The light outside threw shadows on the wall and whoever was outside was really tall and skinny. I was thanking god that the blinds were closed this time—most times they weren't. I got down on all fours and tried to crawl slowly away from the lamp I was praying to god whoever was out there would go away. The doorknob to the door moved and rattled under what seemed to be a very strong hand. I started to breath heavily and I could feel my body heat rise up to its limits. I wanted to knock myself across the head for leaving my cell phone in my room.

I crawled toward the counter near the kitchen to grab the house phone I ran my hand around the counter and found the cradle of the phone; my stomach rolled when I realized the house phone wasn't where it was supposed to be.

"Shit." I smacked my hand against the floor.

BANG!!!!!! The front door flew open with such ease it was like it was never locked. I screamed and flew to the stairs I became the clumsiest chick ever known to man—I tripped over my own two feet and kept stumbling all over the stairs. God I was freaking out I didn't want to be caught by this dark phantom of the night and I was hoping that phantom would not be the man called Victor to finish what he started last night. I made it half way up the stairs in thinking I would make it, but my feet were ripped out from under me. I tried to kick the intruder off of me my foot connected to what felt like his face. He cried out in pain I could hear him fall down the stairs and crash down at the bottom. I knew this was not the same man from before he was much more elegant then this. I managed to yell out at him.

"Get the hell out of my house . . . if you don't I'll call the police!"

"Like . . . hell . . . . you are!"

I freaked when he finally spoke I took my chances and ran to the top of the stairs and into my room. I wasn't too sure if he was running after me, but I wasn't sticking around to find out I slammed my bed room door and locked it. I ran to the side of my bed to get my cell phone and as I snatched it up my first impulse was to dial 911, but instead I grabbed the paper David gave me and dialed the number. The lock on my door was strong enough to hold back the slightest pounding from Tammy, but a fully grown man was a whole different story. The first pound didn't make the door crash to the floor. That gave me time to put the call through it rang twice I didn't expect him to pick up the phone seeing how it was really late and all, I should have called the police. Panic began to build in my stomach and went straight to my chest and into my heart, which by the way was speeding one hundred miles per hour. The tears began to build up on the fourth ring. The second pound made the door whine and shutter as if it were in as much pain as I was. "Hello?"

My heart fluttered when David answered the phone. "Please help me! Someone's trying to break in!"

"I'm on my way Anne just stay put!" The line went dead I buried myself in the corner of my room trying to avoid the worst situation that was happening to me. The third and final pound made the door brake in one spot.

"Oh please leave me alone! Why are you doing this?!" I covered my face because I didn't want to see what was coming for me.

"I'll get you—you're dead girly!" His voice sent me into hysterical cries.

Just then I heard a scream like nothing I have ever heard before. It sent chills running down my spine I put my hands over my ears and closed my eyes as tight as was humanly possible.

My body was pulled up off the floor I screamed and tried to kick away the evil intruder. "Anne! Anne! It's me David!"

I opened my eyes and all the terror and all the frustration of wondering why the hell this was happening to me was pulled away from me and put into a place that was unknown to me.

"Oh David!" I threw my arms around his neck.

"It's okay Anne he's gone." More tears were running down my face.

"Why . . . .

"Don't worry about it Anne it's taken care of." I was shaking and my shoulder was killing me. My life was going to hell. I finished making David's shirt into my own personal tissue and tried to gain my composer, fat chance I could ever do that at the moment. David sat me down on my bed and tried to calm me down by gently stroking my face. It was weird David had this power that I couldn't explain at all. He made me feel at ease at that moment like nothing horrible could ever happen to me.

"Are you okay Anne?" He grabbed my face in between his hands and examined me thoroughly. My body shivered from an unknown draft.

"You're shaking terribly Anne you have to breathe . . . can you do that for me?" I nodded my head in hopes that my lungs were working. I took in one breath, but it felt like I was breathing in poison. This whole mess had my whole entire body freaking out it wasn't functioning right. I had to figure out why that guy was after me.

All the questions I had in my mind came flying out of my mouth without thought or hesitation.

"Why was that guy trying to hurt me?! What did he want from me?! Who the hell did I piss off this time?!"

"Take it easy Anne you're going to have a panic attack if you don't slow down!"

"I don't want to slow down! I want this shit to stop happening to me!" I got up from my bed and moved around David to see how much damage was done to my door—also I didn't know how the hell I was going to explain this one to Dad.

"Do I have a target on my forehead that says 'come and get me'!" This wasn't good I was starting to rant.

"No Anne that's not it at all . . .

"Then what the hell is it David? What makes me any different from the point when my Mom was alive to the point when she wasn't alive?"

The realization of that became so real that it dawned on me—was I meant to die too? "I can't answer your questions Anne."

"Why the hell not?! And you can at least answer that one!" David's face became a dark in the mid hours of the morning.

"Because too much is at stack here Anne, and if I say anything out of the ordinary then something much worse is going to happen, and I will never forgive myself."

David walked around me, and it seemed like he wanted to say something more, but all he did was simply shake his head and walk out of my bed room leaving me completely alone with unanswered questions. I stood there for a moment completely speechless none of this made any sense to me.

"Wait!" I ran through my doorway to the top of the stairs. He was half way out the front door. David turned around; his face was unreadable I couldn't interpret what he was thinking.

"What is it Anne?" David stood there and waited for me to come down the stairs. He was a bit taller than me so I had to standup straighter.

"There's something more about all of this . . . . something about you that I can't really figure out."

"I had a feeling you knew something more about that black rose Anne . . .

David's eyes tore into me they were like powerful beams of light that burned my soul on contact. I had to look away. "Anne if you know what's good for you; you would explain to me what it is that you know. If you don't it will only make things worse for you . . . I feel so connected to you Anne and I think if you just let me in I may be able to understand what exactly is going on . . . . don't make the mistake of not telling me Anne . . . . before it's too late."

"What do you mean before its too late?" David shook his head and walked out.

I couldn't explain anything to David, because I didn't exactly know what was going on either—mumbled dreams and weird visions—how could I explain any of it to David when I didn't know what he was looking for. I slumped my shoulders and spun around to see how bad the house looked. The good thing was it didn't look like a tornado went through the living room. Dad still hadn't shown up which was a relief because I didn't need him to be worried about me; that would make things worse.

I picked up some couch pillows that ended up on the floor maybe the intruder knocked them over which reminded me I had no idea where that guy was. Had David done something to him? I mean that scream was terrible it still gave me chills. I managed to clean up the mess in living room. The front door really wasn't all that damaged under the slightest pressure it would open with ease.

I had to go upstairs and see how much damage was done to my door. I couldn't tell Dad why I had a huge hole in my bedroom door. Something stopped me a ringing noise. "Oh shit!" It was the fucking house phone I had no idea where the hell it was. I ran around the house looking for it I ended up in my Dads room the phone was on his bed. That irritated the shit out of me—speaking of Dad that was who was calling. Boy he had amazing timing.

"Hello."

"Hey Kiddo how's everything going . . . you holding up okay?" I had to lie to him I had no choice.

"Ya everything is okay Dad."

"Are you getting rest Anne it's pretty early for you to be up?"

"Yes I'm getting rest don't worry about me. Are you coming home anytime soon?" I was sick of Dad being worked like a dog.

"I'll be home around nine. Alright kiddo I have to go now I'll talk to you later." Dad hung up and that was the end of that short lived conversation. It was going on seven o'clock in the morning there was no way in hell I was going back to sleep. I walked out of my Dad's room I was extremely tired, but I just didn't care anymore. I walked past the stairs, but at that moment the doorbell rang. "Shit what now?" I was hoping it wasn't anybody from next door it wouldn't be good if they noticed anything strange. I ran down the stairs hoping I wouldn't fall down—I really didn't need to hurt anything else on my body.

The doorbell rang again I made it on the third ring. I opened the door to find Tyler standing there.

"Oh it's you. What do you want?"

"Wow what's up with you?" Can I come in or is there a law stating I can't enter through the front door." I really didn't want Tyler to notice anything off, but if I didn't let him in that would make him even more suspicious about me.

"It's cool you can come in." One thing though I had to keep him from going upstairs. I closed the door behind us and made my way to the couch.

"Something's wrong." Tyler stopped himself from sitting down. I turned my head and faced Tyler.

"What do you mean?" I totally didn't expect Tyler to notice anything off putting.

"I mean it . . . something is really off about you Anne."

"Stop being stupid Tyler there's nothing wrong at all." I was starting to get really nervous.

"You're lying to me Anne I know you are."

"What makes you think I'm lying to you?"

"Because your way to nervous about something."

"No I'm not I'm perfectly fine." I hated that Tyler noticed those things about me honestly it was getting on my nerves.

"Just forget it Tyler nothing is wrong! What do you want anyway?" I was hoping that this would throw Tyler off his trail of annoying curiosity.

"Oh ya . . . . um I think I may have dropped something important in your room last night." Shit I didn't see that one coming I sure as hell didn't want him anywhere near my room. If he was truly becoming suspicious then my broken door was not going to be any help.

"I didn't see anything of yours in my room Tyler." I had honestly didn't see anything at all, but from the look on Tyler's face he was determined to go and look for himself.

"Well then you won't mind me taking a look just to make sure I didn't drop anything." He ran past me and up the stairs.

"No Tyler!" I tried to get ahead of him, but he was way too fast for me. I watched him get to the top of the stairs and turn the corner. The moment had come there was no avoiding this situation at all. When I finally made it Tyler was standing their looking at my door. I could tell he was thinking really hard. I opened my mouth to say something which of course would have been a horrible lie on my part, but he beat me to it.

"Don't say anything Anne. I knew something was wrong but why must you keep trying to hide things from me?"

I couldn't think of a good excuse. All I could do was stare at him and not say anything at all. Tyler turned around and grabbed me by the shoulders it made me wince my shoulder was still killing me.

"What happened here Anne?"

"Nothing happened . . . don't worry about it Tyler." I twisted away from his grip and walked into my room.

"Anne just for once I would like you to talk to me you can't keep everything inside." I grabbed anything that was on the floor and threw it on my bed.

"Could you please stop for a minute Anne?!"

"Why?!"

"Because I want to help you Anne, don't you get that I care about you!"

"I don't need your help Tyler Dawson!" I was throwing more things on my bed but Tyler grabbed me again by the shoulders and spun me around." Again the pain was undeniable.

"Let me go Tyler!"

"No! I know what's going on here and I'm going to save you from this insanity!" I was trying to slap him on the arms but that didn't do a damned thing.

"What do you think you know Tyler?! What makes you think that you can "save" me?!"

"Because I know what he is Anne!" I stopped trying to hit him and became very still.

"What do you mean you know what he is?"

"It's complicated Anne." Tyler still had a hold of me I finally twisted out of his grip.

"How is it fucking complicated Tyler?" I sat down on the edge of my bed.

"Anne you make things so unbearable for yourself and I don't think you realize what you have gotten yourself into."

"Into! What the hell do you mean by that?! Look Tyler I think I've had enough of this."

I got up and stood my ground. "I think it's time for you to go." I crossed my arms around my chest and looked right into Tyler's eyes.

"Is this how it's going to be Anne?"

"Yes it is Tyler."

"Whether you like it or not Anne I'm going to save you from all of this shit!"

"I don't need saving. What I need is for you to leave me alone." Tyler stood their staring down at me as if I would break and tell him that I was the stupid one, and that I needed him more than ever.

"Do you want to know the sad part of this whole messed up situation is Anne?"

"No! But I'm pretty sure you're going to tell me!"

"Damned right I'm going to tell you . . . Anne you won't open your eyes to see what is actually happening to you."

"But . . .

"No Anne I'm not done! I'm sick of being on the sidelines that's where I've been this whole entire time, and I'm fucking tired of it! But not this time Anne no way in hell!"

"Damn it Tyler nothing is going on with me so just stop it already!" Tyler began to laugh in irritation he looked like he was ready to punch a hole in my bedroom wall.

"Anne I'm telling you that I'm not going to stand for this anymore. You're always thinking I can't see anything that goes on with you, but I do, and like I said last night I'm not fucking stupid! So don't stand here and assume that I'll take the shit that's coming out of you damned mouth right now!"

I couldn't believe Tyler was blowing up like this I had never seen him in such a state before, but I couldn't take it from him it was way too hard. I could have taken this from someone else, but with every word that was coming from him was like a razor slicing across my skin and it hurt terribly. I had to defend myself I couldn't let him see me cry out in pain or give up in any way.

"Well you know what Tyler I won't speak to you anymore then that should make things better for us both!" I could tell that stung Tyler as much as it stung me to say it.

"Well that shouldn't really bother me because I'm pretty fucking used to it!" Tyler turned away from me I could barely hear what he was mumbling under his breath.

"You're such a jerk Tyler!"

"Hey!" I turned around to see that Dad was standing in the doorway I hadn't realized how much time passed by.

"Why are you two fighting?" Dad looked concerned.

"Oh hey Dad!" I had no idea what to say to him it was a matter of coming up with a good lie and right now I couldn't come up with one I was stuck in between a rock and a hard place.

"It's nothing Mr. Black me and Anne are just having a slight disagreement nothing we can't handle . . . right Anne?" I was completely shocked Tyler completely covered for me I had no idea why he didn't spill his guts and tell my Dad what was going on.

"Um . . . . ya right everything's fine. You know how teenagers are Dad we get along and in the next second we nearly wanting to rip into each other." I tried to laugh to relieve most of the tension that was between all of us. I looked at Tyler he didn't seem to be amused at all by my weak ass joke.

"That's a comforting thought honey, but you to need to get along I can't have you two "ripping into one another" can we all agree to that ?" I nodded my head in agreement.

"Yes Mr. Black I'll make sure that we both stay in one piece." Tyler grabbed me up into his arms and hugged me. I didn't like it very much, but I had to convince my Dad that nothing was going on. Dad turned to exit my room but stopped and noticed my bed room door. "What happened to your door Anne?" Shit Dad had noticed I had no idea what the hell I was going to say.

"Well you see Dad . . . I was . . . I had nothing not one damned lie that would be good enough for this situation.

"Well spit it out Anne this door wasn't like this when I left." No words would come out of my mouth I was in complete shock.

"I did it Mr. Black." I turned to Tyler I couldn't believe he was admitting to something that wasn't his fault. I looked at Dad he didn't seem to react at first.

"Why would you do something like this Tyler?" I didn't think Tyler would have a good explanation at all, but clearly I was underestimating Tyler big time.

"Well Mr. Black when I came over Anne was complaining that she was locked out of her room. So I had to help out somehow."

"Well I see you don't know how to pick a lock young man." Dad was looking at Tyler sternly. I couldn't believe Tyler was helping me, I mean I really didn't see any point for him to do this for me.

"Can't say I do Mr. Black, you know how we guys do it . . . . we use muscle before brains." Tyler had a big huge smile on his face he seemed to be back to his normal dorky self.

"Well we're going to have to get you a new door Anne . . . one without a lock, that way Mr. Muscle doesn't have to break down anymore doors for this family. Dad walked out of my room without another word. I couldn't believe he bought it.

"You're welcome Anne." Tyler flopped down into my chair and looked up at me. "Why would you do that for me Tyler . . . I mean after everything I said . . . why would you help me?"

"In case you haven't noticed I'm your friend, and I guess I'm just willing to do anything for you Anne." Tyler looked determined.

"I just don't understand you . . . . i don't understand why you care so much."

"Why do you even have to think that way Anne? Don't you see that I have to care . . . . I have to be the one to make sure you don't get hurt in anyway."

"Tyler . . . it's not your burden to bear. What gave you the idea that you had to take on that role?" Tyler got out of my chair and turned to the window with a mournful sigh.

"I just have to okay."

"That's all I'm going to get out of you . . . right?"

"Yup that's pretty much it." Tyler slumped his shoulders and turned to face me.

"Look . . . do you want to get out of here or do you just want to hang out here all day, I mean cause I really don't want to." I wanted an answer so badly, but I knew I wasn't going to get one. I never knew Tyler to be so stubborn; I mean I'm the one who's always stubborn.

"Ya . . . I guess that's a good idea. Go ahead I'll be down in a minute feel free to grab anything out of the kitchen." Tyler left my room in a swift motion I stood there trying to figure out what the hell just happened. I knew Tyler was hiding something from me something that was way beyond our friendship.

Tyler Dawson

I ran down stairs to find Tyler sitting on the kitchen counter waiting for me. "Where do you want to go Tyler?" He looked at me his eyes were distant as if he were lost.

"Are you okay Tyler?"

"Ya I'm fine." I really didn't believe him at all.

"Where were you Tyler?" I walked up to Tyler and looked into his eyes.

"I have no idea what you're talking about I've been right here this whole time." Tyler seemed uncomfortable.

"That's not what I mean Tyler. You looked like you were miles away . . . what were you thinking about?" Tyler turned away from my gaze.

"I wasn't thinking about anything Anne." Tyler hoped off the counter and was heading to my front door. "Hey wait Tyler?"

"Keep up Anne." I looked at my watch it was ten o'clock and I had no idea where Tyler was going to take me. "Okay okay." I snatched my jacket off the chair next to me and we were both out the door . . . .

Tyler's Impala rumbled passed old buildings and people walking to unnamed places.

"So where are we going? Tyler looked at me for a moment then looked away.

"Not too sure yet . . . I just wanted to get out of your house being there was bugging the crap out of me." I could tell Tyler wasn't relaxed at all the knuckles of his hands were so white from his grip on the steering wheel.

"Okay I'm sorry Tyler . . . .

"Don't be sorry it's just how I am . . . I get bothered very easily in tense situations; walking away is what I do best, and when that doesn't work . . . well you really don't want to know what happens." I couldn't help but be a little nervous at this point I couldn't read Tyler.

"Alright I've decided we're going to my house; it's all I can come up with right now . . . you okay with that Anne?" I was in shock at first—never in my life had I ever been to Tyler's house I didn't even know where he lived.

"Uh . . . ya sure I'm okay with that." The palm of my hand was burning because at this point I punctured my fingernails into my skin. This was way too overwhelming for me. I didn't really know too much about Tyler's home life, I mean as kids we never really asked him about it we were just way to busy playing house or some stupid shit like that. And Tyler never really talked about it.

"You look tense Anne." Tyler's voice dragged me out of my thoughts and back into the car.

"What!? No I'm fine . . . really I am Tyler."

"I'm going to call bullshit on that one; I know when you get tense Anne."

"And how do you know when I am Tyler?" I crossed my arms over my chest and slumped into the seat trying to avoid any eye contact as possible.

"That's easy your hands give it away, he grabbed my hand and turned it palm up, see right there you dig your nails into your palm . . . that looks really painful maybe you should stop doing that."

"Okay so I get a little tense . . . that doesn't mean anything, and there's one thing I don't like Tyler and that's being freakin analyzed." I looked up at Tyler.

"It's not analyzing it's something I've noticed about you Anne."

"Well stop noticing . . . okay." Tyler laughed to himself and sighed. I was hoping this conversation was over.

"Well I'll make sure to write that down somewhere . . . that's if I don't forget." I hated Tyler's sarcasm I rolled my eyes and shook my head. The conversation was over and I was really glad that it was—I couldn't take it anymore. At this point I couldn't tell where we were going, I was sure I wasn't anywhere near where I lived. I wanted to ask where we were and how far his house was, But Tyler was already pulling onto a narrow road.

"Up ahead is my house, just give me a minute this damned road is a hassle . . . . Sorry it's a bit bumpy watch your head I don't want you to get injured." I made sure to lower myself down a bit to avoid hitting my head on anything. My shoulder was beginning to hurt again I sure as hell didn't want to hurt that even more, plus I had to make sure Tyler didn't notice anything off, not that he didn't already.

Tyler finally pulled up into a drive way I was in shock it was like looking at a castle. It was beautiful but scary at the same time.

"You live here?" I turned to Tyler; his face seemed to fall in shadow. "Ya I live here . . . shocker right? He turned the keys and pulled them out of the ignition making the car shack a little.

"It's just . . .

"You didn't picture me living in such a place . . . right?" Tyler leaned up against the steering wheel placing his forehead against his hands. I didn't know what to say nothing would come out of my mouth.

"Well I take no offense to your shock, I've never really told anyone about this anyway . . . . let alone bringing anyone here . . . you're the first. Would you like to see the inside or would you rather stay in the car?"

"No I don't want to stay in the car." Tyler opened his car door and pushed himself out of the car slamming the door he left me behind and started walking towards his house. I got out of the car and hesitated for a moment I shook my head and slammed the car door behind me.

"Wait for me Tyler!" Tyler already had the front door opened I stood next to him.

"Welcome to hell." There was that grin again I rolled my eyes and walked inside. "This looks nothing like hell Tyler."

"Ya well you haven't lived here, the surface is nice, but you truly have to look deeper than that."

Wow Tyler that's deep I didn't know you had it in you to be so poetic." I smiled so Tyler would know that I was only joking.

"I do try Anne." Tyler laughed and walked to a room next to us. I tried to get myself to be calm and not so tense and nervous. This situation was very complicated and I just didn't want anything to happen to Tyler. I was a danger to him and anyone else that new me in any way. I hesitantly followed him into the room. Tyler walked across and sat down on a couch in the middle of the room. "You want to sit down?" I took the time to look around the walls were filled with antic paintings and the rest of the furniture was amazing. I felt like I was walking into some amazing store or something.

"I really can't believe this Tyler." I made it to the couch and sat next to Tyler. "How come you never said anything?" Tyler coughed into his hand and sat up a little straighter. "No one ever asked . . . . so I never said anything . . . . if no one asks I won't bring it up it's really not all that important that I tell anyone." He shrugged his shoulders and became quite. "Sounds about right Tyler . . . . so where are your parents?" (Well I couldn't really think of a time that I've ever saw them; it was funny how I never really noticed.) Tyler looked away from me and centered his eyes on something else in the room. "Their dead." Tyler said it so bluntly no emotion was present in his voice just cold hostility. "I'm sorry Tyler I didn't know." Tyler looked back at me and blinked a couple times.

"No big deal Anne it was a long time ago." I wanted to move on so badly I didn't want to bring up anymore bad memories for him.

"So do you live by yourself then?" Hopefully that was a good subject change to get his mind off his parents for a while. It was so weird to know that Tyler didn't have either of his parents I was lucky enough to have my Dad.

"In a way I do I have a uncle who'll stop by every once and awhile to check up on me . . . . you know just to see if I'm doing okay—just to make sure I'm not going crazy in this enormous house." It was strange to find out parts of Tyler's life that I didn't know existed I just really had no idea.

"Wow I can't believe you kept this a secret for so many years without telling me it makes no sense."

"Well Anne it's not something you bring up in a normal conversation, and besides it would have been very selfish of me to bring it up when you were going through a lot with your Mom, and I defiantly wasn't going to bring it up after your Mom died.

"Tyler it wouldn't have mattered because you're my friend it would have gotten my mind off of everything that was going on."

"Even so I don't like spilling my guts out about everything Anne . . . . even if I really wanted to."

"So what the heck is stopping you?" I was becoming very annoyed.

"Ya well you don't tell me everything . . . . so why in the world would I tell you everything?"

Tyler had a good point, but I just couldn't tell him everything I wanted to keep him safe cause I had no idea what was after me.

"Well I guess you're right Tyler."

"Ya I know I am." Ego was ever so present in that last statement.

"So do you want to see the rest of the house or do you want to continue this intriguing conversation?" I was glad Tyler wanted to move on so I nodded my head. He got up from the couch and headed towards an opening at the other side of the living room. I caught up to him, we were in a hallway the walls were filled with paintings and pictures; none of which consisted of happy family memories; just cold dark art.

"I guess your parents were into art?"

"Ya mostly my Dad was, he liked spending his time at museums and I mean the kind you see on movies, and he was a great artist too. Most of these paintings are his and most of them are from trips he took around the country." I was amazed I couldn't believe such talent could come out of a human being. "My mom would always say art was like a second love to him . . . . I figured it would be his first love, but I would never say that to her face. She never quite understood why he loved it so much; I could never really figure it out myself. My Dad spent most of his time in the basement creating his next master piece." I couldn't help wondering if Tyler picked up any of his Dad's talents.

"Do you paint Tyler?" He turned to look at me. "I used to . . . . but after my parents died . . . . so did my love for painting."

"I'm sorry." I felt sad I began to feel tears form into my eye's they spilled over and I quickly wiped them away. We moved on to the next floor. "How could you still live here Tyler?"

"You're kidding me right where the hell do you think I would go?" We stopped in the middle of the hall way.

"Well . . . . I don't know I mean I don't think I could stay in a house where most of my life I lived with my parents . . . . the pain would be too much. I have a hard time waking up in my parent's house, because I feel like at any moment my Mom would come into my room and wake me up for breakfast, but I know she won't. What makes it easier I guess is having my Dad their . . . . if I didn't have him I wouldn't be strong enough to stay in the house I grew up in . . . without them."

Tyler was staring at me like he was seeing me for the first time. "Anne . . . I can't leave this house I'm bound to it." I could hear the sorrow in his voice and it broke my heart. Tyler lowered his gaze and walked pass me to open a door behind me he stuck his hand in and flicked on a light.

"Welcome to my own little prison it's not much, but heck it's my room." Tyler grabbed my hand and led me into his room. Everything was clean I wasn't expecting that at all. There was a massive bed at the center of his room and a dresser filled with paints and brushes cluttered on top of it. The question popped out of my mouth before I could stop it.

"Why did you keep all the paints Tyler?"

He let go of my hand and turned to look at his long and forgotten paints and brushes, it's as if he sent those to the grave as well.

"I don't care about it anymore; I haven't touched those since they both died." Tyler turned away and moved to a different part of his room. "So what do you care about then Tyler?"

"Hell if you don't know the answer to that question already then your one heck of a blind girl." Tyler smiled to himself a little I hadn't seen him smile since this morning—which is odd for him because he's always seemed to smile all the time.

"Hey I take offense to that I'm neither blind nor stupid."

"I didn't say you were stupid just blind." I had no idea where he was going with this. The whole damned day was weird as hell, and it wasn't getting any better.

"I would feel better if we change the subject." I turned away from Tyler I wanted to avoid what seemed to be his way of sharing his feelings about me. "I will talk about this weather you like it or not." I had this feeling of punching him across the face, but I didn't think it would be smart.

"Just drop it Tyler!" I swung around to face him.

"What the fuck for!? You always think you can boss me around Anne, but I'm no push over I have feelings to Anne." I know you're not a push over Tyler but it's just I don't feel like this is the best time for this . . . . I don't know what you want from me Tyler." he was making it hard to just be friends. What I didn't understand was why he felt this way about me . . . well in anyway it made no sense.

Well hell Anne I don't want much from you—but what I do want is for to listen to me and give me a chance to take care of you." Tyler walked up to me and grabbed my hand.

"Will you let me take care of you Anne?" Tyler held my hand in a tight grip.

"I just don't know right now Tyler . . ." He let go of my hand and that gave me a chance to give us some space—I glanced at the paints and brushes. "Can I see one of your paintings then?" I thought it was worth a try, and besides we weren't getting anywhere else. I waited for his answer expecting him to say hell no.

"Their right behind the dresser in that case . . . . have at it." Tyler moved to lean up again his bedroom wall; his eyes were serious and unreadable." Um . . . okay." I moved around the dresser and found a black case I pulled it out and placed it on his bed. "Um I really don't want to open it why don't you Tyler . . . .

"No you go ahead I haven't touched those in years I'm not going to start now."

"Okay . . . . I opened the flap to his case and grabbed one of the canvases out of its little prison. I couldn't believe it it was as if the painting were alive it seemed like the colors and shapes were moving it was a wonderful.

"Wow that's amazing Tyler." I didn't understand why someone could possibly stop such a talent.

"Ya well I'm nothing like my Dad he was the real artist."

"Even so you're still good you share your Dad's talent Tyler."

"Thank god that's the only thing I share from my Dad." I couldn't really imagine what Tyler's parents were like, but the way he described them they sounded so cold. Tyler pushed himself off the wall and sat at the other side of his bed. I pulled out another canvas it took me by surprise. "Why did you paint this Tyler?" He looked up and stared straight at his painting. "There are many reasons why I painted that one . . . . at that point of my life you were the only thing that got me through my parent's death, so I panted you." I looked at the painting again—did I really look like that, innocent and lost. I placed the canvases back into their case and dug into my pocket to glance at my cell phone. The time had gone by fast it was going on noon; Dad would be up by now.

"I think maybe you should take me back home Tyler." Tyler looked up at me it took a minute for him to respond.

"Why are you in a hurry Anne?"

"I'm not in a hurry; I just think I should go home . . . . you know just to see if my Dad is okay."

"Well if this were any other time I would believe you, but this isn't any other time so I don't believe you." Tyler pushed himself off his bed and placed himself in front of me.

"Why in the world would you say such a thing like that Tyler?" I was starting to feel like there was some sort of challenge to say something wrong, that way he could find a reason to be right.

"Because you want to avoid me Anne, and your using your Dad as an excuse to get yourself out of it." I hated the way he could read me so well it got on my damned nerves. "I'm not avoiding anything . . . . just as Tyler was about to protest, but my cell phone rang I was saved and I thanked god for it. Tyler looked at me in a strange way I dug my phone out of my pocket and checked the screen . . . . it was my Dad.

"It's my Dad Tyler."

"Ya sure whatever Anne." I flipped my phone open and answered.

"Hey Dad."

"Anne honey I need you to come home right now." I didn't like the tone in my Dad's voice.

"Are you okay Dad?"

"Ya I'm fine Anne I just want you to come home."

"Okay . . . . Tyler is going to take me home."

"Alright just be careful." I heard a click on the other end of the phone then a dial tone I flipped my phone shut and stuck it back in my pocket. Dad sounded weird I couldn't read his voice, but I did know something was off.

"I have to go Tyler."

"Ya I got it the first time you said it Anne—I'll take you home." Tyler grabbed me by the arm and walked me right out of his house not saying one word. It was hard to make out what Tyler was feeling at the moment. I didn't want to ask I watched Tyler get into his car . . . . I followed shortly.

The Drive Home

It couldn't have been more awkward Tyler wouldn't say a word to me not one. From what I could tell we were an hour away from my house way to long for me to handle. I needed music something to save me from this silent torture. I was praying for something anything at all.

"We really need to talk Anne." I shook my head and slumped into my seat—I guess I prayed a little too hard.

"I don't want to talk Tyler."

"Well guess what we're going to talk no if ands or buts about it Anne." God I didn't want this.

"What do you want from me Tyler?!"

"I want you to talk to me!"

"Why is it so important for me to open up?"

"Because Anne . . . . you mean everything to me, I realized that when we were kids to . . . . I was there for you when you're Mom got sick, and I'm still here for you now, so please don't act as if I don't give a damn Anne."

"I know you've been there for me—and I thank you for that . . . . but there are certain things that I can't tell you."

"God Damn it Anne! Why do you keep trying to protect me, it's not your job it never was. Stop trying so hard to put up those walls to protect me!" Tyler was starting to speed it was making me really nervous.

"Tyler could you please slow down!"

"Sorry . . . ." Tyler was mad I could tell that by the speeding alone; everyone knew when Tyler would get mad—he would run to his Impala and race down the roads like a speed demon straight out of hell.

"It's okay Tyler . . . . just try not killing us . . . .

"You know Anne now's not the time to be freakin funny."

"Just take me home safely okay I really need to see if my Dad is okay. I didn't like the way he sounded on the phone."

"See right there your trying to change the subject . . . . you always do that I'm getting really sick of it Anne."

"Ya well get used to it Tyler, because this is how I'll always be you either learn to love it—or don't—doesn't matter to me." I had no idea where that came from, but the way I said it had more power in it than anything I'd ever said to Tyler.

"Fine." That was that Tyler stopped talking, but I didn't like the way this conversation ended. I was losing him I could feel our friendship slipping this wasn't the way I wanted to lose Tyler. I wanted to protest to tell him everything was fine, that nothing was wrong with me and everything would be okay; but I knew that was a lie I knew everything wasn't okay, that everything was falling apart in my world, and I knew that I was losing my best friend. The whole thing was wrong I wanted to scream and cry, and god forbid beat the crap out of something, but I knew that wouldn't solve anything. I knew that I was keeping Tyler safe by not telling him what happened with me and Victor, if I told him anything about that I knew he would do something stupid—that was Tyler 'think later do something stupid instead' that was why I had to protect him.

We it made to my house an hour later a dark blue unmarked vehicle was parked in the drive way, that made my blood run very cold. Something bad happened I knew that at that very second. Tyler parked beside the cop car and got out of the car without a word; I followed shortly. Tyler and I ran up the porch in haste—Tyler took the liberty to knock on the door before I could get my key out of my pocket.

"You know anything about this Anne?" Tyler looked at me curiously.

"Can't say I really do Tyler?"

"Ya well I don't like this one bit, if you got anything to tell me now would be the best time to talk." The front door opened before I could get the next words out. Dad was standing in the doorway his gray eyes were faded his face was unshaven and his black hair was messy.

"Oh Anne darling I'm glad your home." Dad grabbed me up in his arms and hugged me tightly. I couldn't breath, but I got the next question out just fine.

"What's wrong Dad?" He put me down and invited Tyler in.

"I was worried something would have happened to you Anne."

"Why would anything happen to me? Clearly I'm fine and in one piece Dad."

"Thank god for that. Why don't you two come sit down in the living room . . . . I'll be with you shortly the Detective's will fill you in."

"What do you mean Detective's . . . . why are they here?" I looked at my Dad with fear.

"Just go to the living room you two I'll be there in a sec." I was starting to get really nervous about the whole thing. We both walked into the living room, the two Detective's were sitting down on the living room couch. Both of them looked up from their notepads and looked us over before one of them spoke.

"Hi you must be Anne I'm Detective John Miller and this is Detective Peter Montero." He pointed to his partner, they both had friendly faces and they both seemed a little too young to be Detective's I didn't understand why that was. John got up from his spot on the couch offering his hand to shack—he was taller than Tyler. I shook John's hand. Would you two take a set; we would like to ask you a couple of questions regarding a particular incident."

"Um okay . . . . I hesitantly took a set on the couch opposite the Detective's Tyler followed closely behind. John cleared his throat before saying anything. "Earlier today we got a call from a local resident, stating he heard a dispute earlier this morning. Now he also stated that the incident accrued close to this area." I was screwed, and I knew it—I didn't know if I could lie to them I was hoping none of the neighbors heard anything, but I should have known better.

"So the question is—did you see anything maybe even heard anything by any chance Anne—you're Father said you were home alone, he also said you haven't been sleeping." Crap I was in shock the words wouldn't come out of my mouth not one freakin word. Johns' face became more businesslike; if I didn't answer his question he would know something was up.

"I . . . . ugh . . . . no I didn't see anything or hear anything." Tyler took his turn to speak which was good because all eyes would be off me, and I could take the time to come up with an almost perfect lie.

"What exactly is it that happened?" Tyler was curious I could see that instantly; he wanted to find out himself if it had anything to do with me. And if it did he wanted more than anything to question me endlessly until I cracked under the pressure.

"Well Peter and I took the call, and headed down here—John looked at his partner and hesitated only for a moment—what we found was not what we expected." John was in deep thought I could tell he was going back to the scene of whatever it was he saw.

"What did you find?" Tyler was at the edge of the couch eager to find out what it was that happened. John cleared his throat again.

"Well we found a man literally in a heap of earth like something just threw him there with so much force—I couldn't explain how such a thing could have happened, let alone what could have done it . . . it couldn't have been a person no one could ever be that strong to throw a full grown man that deep into the ground." God I was trying not to shack, but I knew instantly who that man was, but what I couldn't explain was how he ended up that way.

"So Anne you're sure you didn't hear anything . . . . nothing at all?" John was trying so hard to get something out of me something he could work with to explain what had happened that morning.

"No I didn't I swear I didn't." I was hoping that sounded truthful. Both John and Peter looked me as if they were trying to mentally get the truth out of me. Dad walked into the living room before anything else could be said. He seemed to have fixed himself up a little bit, but I could still see in his eyes that he was extremely worried.

"So I take it you told them what happened." The Detectives took there gazes of me and focused on my Dad.

"Yes Mr. Black, but it seems your daughter doesn't know anything, but if she does come up with anything—anything at all give us a call so we can set up a meeting at our precinct to talk." John tapped Peter on the shoulder I guess that signaled something between them. They both got up from the couch shook my Dad's hand, and gave him a card to call them at any time of day if anything came up. Tyler and I were left in the living room while my Dad escorted the Detective's outside.

I was nervous I wasn't too sure if John believed me, if he had he wouldn't have left a card with my Dad. I couldn't lie that was for sure, Tammy could lie she had a talent for it—I only wish I had that kind of talent.

"You know . . . ." crap Tyler was ready to grill me I knew that for sure Tyler knew I was lying he could see right through me when I did.

"I swear I didn't see anything Tyler . . . .

"So how the hell do you explain the massive hole in your bedroom door?"

"That I can't explain to you Tyler . . ." I got up from the couch and walked to living room window I looked out to see my Dad talking to the Detective's.

I could hear Tyler getting up from the couch. "Alright you won't tell me . . . that's fine, but I am eventually going to find out myself and you can't stop me Anne . . . nothing you can say to me will change my mind." The threat was calm, calmer than anything I've ever heard from Tyler. I didn't like it at all he was scaring me; I would have preferred him to yell at me. I turned around and looked at Tyler I could see in his eyes that he had a plan brewing, and he wasn't going to give up on it.

Dad walked into the living room I hadn't heard him open the front door.

"Did I just miss something—looks like you two are ready to get into it."

"No sir everything is fine Anne and I have just come to an understanding." I looked up at Tyler he was determined to do what he had to do to find out what was going on with me. Dad just nodded his head and shrugged his shoulders he didn't want to ask any questions as to what Tyler was talking about. "Well now that that's done, I'll go prepare something for dinner your welcome to stay Tyler." Dad walked to the kitchen ending the conversation.

Tyler looked at me with a smug smile on his face he yanked off his jacket and tossed it on the couch, he was going to stay. I think what he had in mind was to keep a sharp eye out on me, and staying for dinner was going to be part of that plan. I crossed my arms over my chest and rolled my eyes. Tyler walked towards the kitchen.

"Would you like some help Mr. Black? Dad popped his head out from the kitchen, and looked at Tyler.

"Ya grab the phone on the couch and order a pizza everything's frozen."

"Great pizza night!—I love pizza!" Tyler grabbed the phone off the couch and started dialing. It seemed like he was back to his happy self, but I knew he was setting his plan in the back of his mind.

I heard a knock on the front door I looked outside the window to see David's car out on the drive way. God I couldn't believe it this couldn't be happening my heart was racing. I went to the door and opened it David was standing their looking as if nothing had happened that very morning. He was wearing his leather jacket again paired with blue jeans and a black shirt.

"Hi." I stood there for a second hesitating whether or not I should let him in.

"Hi David." Dad was right behind me he moved me aside, and let David in. I fallowed them out of the hall and to the living room. "How have you been?" Dad sat in his chair and David took a set on the couch.

"I've been fine." David looked at me with a questioning gaze. Tyler walked in from the kitchen—phone in hand he looked up and was about to say something when his gaze fell on David. Tyler's face grew dark it didn't look like he was happy to see David.

"Get a hold of a pizza place Tyler? Dad was looking at Tyler, but he didn't seem to hear my Dad. Hey Tyler did you hear me?" Tyler snapped out of it and looked at my Dad.

"Ya I got a hold of a place, pizza should be here in a few." Tyler walked across the living room, and sat on the opposite couch of Tyler. I was still standing I came to a realization that I had to choose who to sit next to. I decided to keep standing. Dad was the first to speak up again.

"So David . . . did you happen to get the news of what happened here in our very neighborhood?"

David looked at my Dad, and didn't hesitate to answer him. "Yes I did the man that was hurt was brought to my hospital, he's in critical condition, and hasn't woken up as of yet."

"That's horrible well I hope the old man pulls through . . . . well I couldn't tell if he was old there was too much dirt covering him. Doesn't matter just as long as he pulls through." Dad seemed to be content about the man being alive, but still seemed to be worried.

"Yes Mr. Black we're hoping he gets well to." David looked at me while he said that.

The doorbell went off I nearly screamed, but held it in. "I'll get it!" I took the chance to run to the door just to give me a reason to get out of the living room. I opened the door and the smell of pizza hit my noise.

"Hi." The pizza guy seemed to be friendly. "Here are your two pizzas and coke—that will be twenty four-thirty."

"I got it." Dad pushed the door opened and gave the guy the money. "Go set the table honey I got it from here." I walked back into the living room—David was still sitting where Dad left him—I didn't know where Tyler disappeared too.

"Need help with anything Anne?" David got up from the couch. I walked the rest of the way to the kitchen. The kitchen was big enough for about three people to stand in; the dining room was adjacent to the kitchen.

"Um . . . . no I think I can handle this on my own." I opened the cabinets to get some plates out. My shoulder was still bothering me the weight of the plates made my arm give a little bit. David was their just in time before one of them landed on the floor.

"Thanks." David grabbed the plates out of my hands and put them on the dining room table.

"I see your shoulder is still bothering you." David stood beside me while I grabbed the cups out of another cabinet.

"It's fine David . . . .

"Maybe I should look at it again just to see if I missed anything."

"Ya right Doctor—you missing anything—I highly doubt that." I smiled just a little bit.

"Very funny Anne . . . I should still look it over . . . .

"Look what over?" I nearly dropped a cup from the sound of Tyler's voice. I turned around to see Tyler leaning against the wall.

"Oh nothing . . . just a paper I wrote for school I wanted him to check it for me." David didn't say anything I guess he figured I had to be lying for a good reason.

"That true David?" David looked at Tyler, but it didn't seem like David was fazed or even slightly nervous.

"Yes it's true; Anne seems to be worried." Tyler didn't seem like he was buying it. Not another word was spoken when my Dad entered the kitchen.

"Who's ready to eat?"

"I am." Tyler took his place at the table.

"You're welcome to join us David." Dad placed the boxes of pizzas down on the table and pulled out a chair for David.

"I guess I could stay for a little while." David pulled off his leather jacket and placed it on the back of the chair. I grabbed all of the cups and placed them on the table. Tyler was glaring at David in between two bites of his pizza, I shook my head. Dad took his place at the end of the table. I was the only one left standing again I looked at my Dad then at David then to Tyler. "I'm not hungry you guys enjoy." Dad gave me a worried look.

"Are you okay Honey?"

"Yes I'm fine Dad."

I ran out of the dining room through the living room snatched my jacket off the hook by the door and ran out the front door jumping the steps all at once. It was getting a little cold outside I wrapped my jacket closer to my body—walking to the old tire swing Mom and Dad put up for me ages ago; I could remember how much I enjoyed being pushed on it. I could hear the faded laughter in the wind as I pushed the tire swing with my finger. A tear escaped and landed on my cheek I wiped it away I knew crying wouldn't get me anywhere, but I could never get myself to stop crying.

"Hey . . . . I turned around to see David standing with his arms crossed.

"Ugh I just wasn't hungry . . . .

"Ya I figured that much when you ran out Anne." David closed the space between us.

"I know you're going through a lot Anne and I'm sorry that a lot of bad things are happening, but I promise I'll be their every step of the way."

"I miss her David." I felt like giving up—just to lay down and let everything bad do whatever the hell it wanted to do to me.

"Miss her Anne it's your right too, this is how you're going to coup . . . to accept your Mom's death."

"Accept her death?" . . . . I almost laughed at the idea of such a concept. You're kidding me right? I'm never going to accept her death not ever. Death is something I will never understand it's awful . . . don't you see that? How could anyone think it's okay for someone they love to just suddenly die . . . it's painful, and I can't ever get rid of that pain." I turned my back to David I didn't want him to see me crying.

"I'm sorry Anne."

"Why are you sorry?" David grabbed my hand and turned me around to face him.

"Because until now I didn't know how much you were hurting, I should have seen it. You're a special person Anne, you have a different view on life, most people would just morn for a little while, but you . . . . you look at death as if it's a poison and not many look at it that way."

"I can't help it—it's in my heart to feel this way." David pulled me into his arms and hugged me. It felt safe to be in his arms, I let myself go and hugged him back tears were flowing from my eyes.

"That man they found . . . . was it the same man who attacked me in my house." I kept my head down so he couldn't see my face.

"Don't worry about that Anne—it's been taken care of." I could feel his arms go ridged against my back.

"Did you do what they said happen to that man?" David pulled himself away from me and avoided looking at me.

"I said don't worry about it Anne it's been handled you don't ever have to worry about that man coming around here anymore I made sure of that."

"What do you mean you handled it?" I walked up to him and touched his arm. David looked at me his eyes were on fire and his face was stern. David wasn't going to tell me anything I could tell by the way he was looking at me.

"I think you better go inside Anne its getting cold."

"Stop telling me what to do David." I was getting really tired of people thinking they could tell me what to do. The only one I would take that crap from was my Dad and that's when I would choose to listen to him. David shook his head showing that he disapproved of my stubbornness.

"Hey you two get inside. I looked to the porch to see Dad standing there. I don't want you guys to be out here at night at least not for a while." Dad went back inside leaving us alone again.

"I should be getting along anyway; I have to get back to the hospital." David turned away from me and started walking to his car.

"Hey! I ran to catch up to David. I wanted to thank you for saving my life—twice it seems." David smiled at me got into his car and started the engine. Before leaving he lowered his window.

"I promised to be their every step of the way and I mean every step." The window went up to his car and he drove away leaving me alone outside. It was funny how I had two people watching me. I took a moment to look at the home I lived in for so many years it seemed to have changed—like a piece of the house had died to. The wind started to pick up and for some reason chills went down my spine I knew more change was going to happen, but right now I just couldn't figure it out. I shook the feeling away and ran up the porch steps and into my house.

Tyler was still in the kitchen drinking his soda. "Where's the Doc?" There was sarcasm noted in that question.

"David had to leave . . . . something about having to go back to the hospital.

"Ya whatever." I rolled my eyes and chose not to say anything to Tyler.

"So what were you two talking about out there?" Tyler looked a bit annoyed.

"Nothing he just wanted to see if I was okay."

"That looked like more than checking if you were okay Anne." I could feel my cheeks go hot; I couldn't believe Tyler was watching us.

"It was nothing Tyler?"

"Sure that's believable . . . . I should get going, when you feel the need to be a little more honest with me give me a call." Tyler walked out of the kitchen and out the front door not saying another word. I could hear the engine to his car start—Tyler took off like he always did fast and leaving dust behind him.

Dream

Let me go! She's dying! Why are you doing this?! . . . ANASTASIA DON'T YOU DARE DIE ON ME!

"There's nothing you can do . . . she's going to die weather you like it or not. This life you want won't happen you're meant for better and bigger things. A life with her will mean nothing."

"How can you now that . . . I love her . . . You don't know anything!"

"Death is all that comes out of human beings . . . nothing more. Understand that this thing . . . this person that you have an infatuation with is merely a pawn in our world . . . that will eventually fade away."

"I will kill you! Do you understand me! I will hunt you down and make you suffer! You were my friend my brother . . . and now you have damned yourself!"

A Pain woke me up from my dream. My stomach felt like it was burning. On top of that my shoulder was still killing me. I rolled out of bed to walk around to see if that would settle down my stomach. My dream felt so real I felt like I was there and the faces were beginning to become a little clearer, but I still couldn't make them out. I shook my head to clear the fuzziness of sleep and stress and realized it was really early, and it dawned on me that it was Monday. School was something that wasn't on my mind. I knew Dad would freak out if he found out I was skipping school, but I really didn't feel like being grilled by anyone especially Tammy she'd grill me like she grills her tofu. "Yuck!" I hadn't seen her in while, yesterday was crappy Tyler was pissed at me, and David was mysterious in so many ways. Dad was still really worried he couldn't get his mind off the poor guy that was hurt not far from our house; if Dad only new that that poor guy tried to hurt me. I knew what I had to do I had to get out of here away from those I loved before any of them got hurt.

Getting dressed was the easiest part, but packing my stuff was the hardest part. I really didn't know what to take with me. Believe me I wasn't really a pro at running away from home, but I thought it would be worth a try. I finally packed most of my clothes into my black suite case and decided it would be best to leave a note—it would be the polite thing to do. The note only took two seconds to write and I was out the door I didn't even know if Dad was home, but in no time he would notice that I was gone. Last night gave me a good reason to leave I'd never experienced anything so violent and unreal in my whole entire life. Only in my dreams that is. My blue Honda was still parked in the same spot David had parked it in I hadn't used my own car not since that night. I threw all my stuff into the back of the car and ran to the driver's side. I never knew it would come to this, but there was no reason for me to stick around this town anymore. I knew I had to make one stop first.

I pulled up to Hill cemetery and took two deep breaths before I entered the grounds. My Mom's tomb stone was still covered in long grass. I still hated the fact that no one would give the dead a second thought. I looked around and the cemetery looked like hell—no pun intended, but seriously why wouldn't anyone take care of this place. There had to be someone around to clean up the place. I decided to take a look around to see if anyone was around maybe a caretaker. I could tell him that he needed to clean the place up a bit.

There wasn't a building in site yet, but I really wanted to find someone. There were so many tombstones I never realized how many people died it never really crossed my mind.

I remembered that David was here at the cemetery, and wondered why he would be here. I walked around for quite some time I didn't know where I was going I finally found myself in a whole different part of the cemetery.

I came across a clearing there appeared to be a stone angel and a tombstone just ahead of me. I decided it wouldn't hurt to take a look at who was buried in such a special part of the cemetery. I walked carefully making sure I wouldn't stumble on anything.

The angel was beautiful and the tomb stone seemed to be made of marble—I walked closer to get a better look a branch blocked the front of the tombstone, I grabbed the branch and moved it carefully away from the stone I knelt down on one knee and looked at the face of the stone.

There seemed to be a portrait of a women but I couldn't tell what she looked like I brushed my hand over it to clear the dirt off of it—my heart stopped—I couldn't believe what I was seeing the portrait of the women looked like me.

"You found her . . . took you awhile to figure it out." My thoughts froze I knew that voice—it was the same menacing voice from the night before. I turned around slowly. You know when I first saw you I thought I was seeing a ghost. But when I caught your scent in the wind it was like being pulled back in time. I didn't know God would be so cruel to bring you back. It's a shame that I have to get rid of you" I was still knelt down on my knee, but I felt like I could make a run for it.

"Okay . . . one . . . I don't know what you're talking about, and two I would love for you to leave me alone." I stood up to see if that would make me feel any better, but it really didn't, Victor was much bigger than me.

"Well that may be . . . but you see I can't leave you alone. David and I have unfinished business to attend to, and I can't have you distracting him any longer."

"Okay then . . . I really think I should be leaving now, I wasn't really planning on staying in this town anyway. Well . . . um . . . hope to never see you again." I tried walking pass Victor, but he put his arm up to block my way.

"Oh I don't think you understand . . . I have to kill you . . . Anastasia."

Chills went down my spine I had never told anyone about my dream and for him to call me by that name was all kinds of wrong. I couldn't take it anymore I ran away.

"Hey . . . where are you going?! We have much to discuss my dear Anastasia!"

Sticks and branches scratched me up pretty good as I ran passed them. I tripped a couple of times and ended up hitting my shoulder on a nearby tree the same damned shoulder. It caused pain to run down my arm. I stopped in my tracks to find myself in front of a building I didn't hesitate I ran to the door, and banged my fists on the wood in hopes that there would be someone inside.

"Help! Please let me in!" I could tell there was someone inside I could here them walking around. Rustling noises were coming from behind me I tried banging on the door harder.

"There's no point . . . he won't be coming out of there, made him a deal that he couldn't refuse. Anyone coming through the cemetery is mine and if he refused he would become part of the cemetery just like everyone else. You won't be gaining anything by running away." Victors voice sounded animal like I didn't want to look at him I still had my hands on the door they were really red from banging against it.

"Please . . . leave me alone." I could hear him chuckle to himself. Victor was enjoying this I could tell, bile was beginning to form in my throat. Victor grabbed my shoulder and turned me around which made my vision spin a bit.

"See me and David are meant to be together, but for some reason David didn't understand that not then and it seems not now either—and it seemed to me that he would never get sloppy after the incident that accrued such a long time ago. But he did and now I'm going to enjoy the time we're going to spend together. What do you think about that?

Victor's eyes were beginning to glow red and at that point I didn't know what to do.

"I . . . uh . . .

"Leave her alone Victor or you will regret it!" David was standing a few paces away from me and Victor.

"Or what David . . . you're going to kill me. I'm tired of your empty threats David. When are you ever going to own up to anything you say?"

"David . . . please help me." My voice was shaky I wanted to cry, but I was way too scared to.

Victor pulled me down from the porch by the arm and I nearly fell to my knees.

"Is this a game to you Victor to screw with my life?!"

"No . . . no games . . . more like a plan that's all. I'm tired of being in the shadows. I feel that it's time we had a chance to take our place in this world.

"No Victor we can be more then shadows . . . . can't you see that we don't have to be monsters!"

"We are monsters David!" Trust me being thrown against a tree is very damaging to the body I tasted blood in my mouth and realized that my lip had busted open I had scrapes all over my arms from the tree. I could hear growling coming from David I looked at him his fists were clinched so tight that the skin on his knuckles appeared to be ripping.

"Boy your anger has gotten worse throughout the years David. But do you have any bite to go with that anger of yours?" Victor seemed to be enjoying himself. I managed to roll on my back the scene that formed in front of me was of pure violence. Victor's face changed into pure anger, and his eyes were the color of crimson. "Get up Anne—run!" That's all I needed no questions asked I got up stumbled a little and took off running. I never knew I could run so fast, but I got to my car faster than I had ever before. I practically flew into my car jammed the keys into the ignition and floored it. I was shaking and crying my lip was still bleeding and the scrapes on my arms were stinging like hell. Forget the shoulder that was damned to hell already.

My head was throbbing with pain I couldn't think straight I almost rammed my car into a tree. There was a load bang on the side of my car I nearly screamed I plowed onto my breaks my head was the next thing to be busted open at least that's what it felt like. Next thing I knew I was being held in strong arms.

My vision began to swim David's face became blurry. "Anne look at me don't close your eyes! Too late I blacked out.

The Whole Truth

My head swam with images of the women that looked like me. She was running and she looked so happy. Anastasia ran and stumbled into opened arms I couldn't see his face his back was facing my point of view. The man picked up Anastasia by the waist and spun her around his face came into view . . . . I couldn't believe it . . . The man I saw in my dreams was David . . . Alexander was David. *Suddenly I was pushed into a different vision. Anastasia was standing in a doorway. Her hair was down and she looked like she was in shock. She finally walked through the doorway in what looked like a bedroom.*

The scene changed and I was looking through Anastasias' point of view. Alexander had one leg out the bedroom window and the other leg was still in the bedroom. Alexander face was changed somehow I couldn't tell what was changed about his face, but he was beautiful. Alexander pulled his other leg inside the room. Alexander adjusted himself and made a coughing noise. He was standing up so straight that he looked like a statue. Anastasia walked up to him without hesitation, and stared right up into Alexander's eyes. They stood there in complete silence for a while. Alexander was the first one to look away he looked like he was in pain. His eyes were glowing an intense green as if they were on fire.

"Don't look at me Anne I'm hideous." That was the first time I ever heard my name fall from Alexander's lips. Anastasia lifted her hands and gently touched Alexanders' face. He leaned into her touch.

"I knew there was something different about you, but I was always told I had an over active imagination, but I always knew nobody could tell me any different."

"I couldn't tell you Anne . . . I thought maybe if I left you that maybe you could have a normal life, but when you walked in here you didn't run away or scream. You didn't yell to your Father that there was a monster in your room.

You don't fear me which is odd. I'm in love with you even more then when you didn't know you were running around with a vampire."

"*I love you with all my heart I don't care what you are.*" Anne closed the space between them. *You are the man I want to spend the rest of my life with. This face . . . this part of you is just as wonderful as any other part of you. I'll always see the man I love in you always.* Anastasia ran her thumb over Alexander's lips he shook from that simple touch. Alexander released a sigh; his lips parted a bit and I could just see the tips of his fangs.

"*Anne you don't know what you're getting yourself into."* Alexander rested his forehead on hers and closed his eyes.

"*I think I know what I'm doing.*" Anne pulled herself up and softly kissed David on his lips. She pulled away and looked into Alexander's eyes.

"*Why did you do that?"*

"*Because I love you Alexander.*" Alexander pulled her closer to him and kissed her.

The scene faded and I woke up coughing trying to pull myself together. Anne are you okay? I realized I was laying on the ground right next to my car. David was holding me in his arms I looked up at him; and said only one word that came to mind.

"Alexander . . . David flinched and seemed to be in shock.

"How . . . how do you know that name?"

David held me tighter.

"I remember . . . !"

I didn't know if that was a good idea to shout out but I really didn't know what to do at that moment. I didn't know whether to jump, scream or just run away.

"I remember you . . . I loved you . . . we loved each other! Your face . . . your voice have been hunting my dreams . . . our memories . . . I really don't know what to call them!"

"Wait . . . you remember . . . but how?!"

The muscles in David's jaw seem to tense up.

"I really don't know how, but every time I came near you these dreams or visions seem to get stronger . . .

An image of my death flashed into my vision . . . my stomach began to twinge in pain.

"Anne are you okay!!"

"You think you would get tired of asking me that." I leaned up against my car to take in a breath.

"Something happened to me didn't it? Victor killed me right? . . . He killed me right in front of you and there was nothing you could do about it."

David began to pace. "How do you remember Anne . . . its impossible?"

"Nothing really is impossible in my life . . . I get that now. But what I really want to know is why would Victor still be after me . . . what have I done so wrong . . . how could I be such a problem for him? I don't care that you're a vampire.

As I said this, the look on David's face changed to distress.

"You remember that part . . . that I'm a vampire."

"Of course that's not something that would be left out." David's face was overcome with shame.

"I think it would be better if we talked about this somewhere else." David seemed to be occupied by something.

"David . . . what's wrong?"

"I just really think we should go."

David grabbed my arm and took me to the passenger side of my car.

"Get in the car." David sounded so stern.

"But . . . David held up his hand to stop me from saying another word.

"Get in the car right now." Everything was changed about David. The way he sounded was nothing I ever experienced before. I got in the car and slammed the passenger side door as hard as possible. David was already in the seat next to me. I yelped from the shock of how fast he was.

"You know every time you appeared out of nowhere I should have guessed what you were . . . . you opened my memories when I went to the hospital that night."

"That's the least of our problems right now Anne." David jammed my keys into the ignition and started the car. David's hands were firmly planted on the steering wheel. David was looking straight ahead as if something had just appeared. I looked up to see Victor standing there he appeared to have no mark on him as if there was no fight at all.

"Okay . . . let's get the hell out of here!"

Victor's smile grew wider to show sharp long daunting fangs. He knew that I was scared and he was enjoying every minute of it. David slammed his foot into the gas pedal and speed toward Victor. I started to freak out as I realized what David was about to do. I put my hands over my face so I wouldn't see the destruction.

"Shit!" I could tell David was really pissed. Then I realized there was no impact. "What happened?" I turned around to look out the back window and turned back to face David. "Where did he go?"

"Fucking bastard deserves die!"

Questions

The few hours that passed between us were filled with silence. I didn't know if it would be best to talk to David, who might I add looked like he was ready to kill something. I really wanted to ask where we were going. There were a lot of questions circling in my mind and I wanted to find out most of the answers behind them.

The sky had an odd color it had a hint of red and black which kind of freaked me out a little. It seemed that the sky's throat was ripped opened to spill throughout the sky. I had to look away it was too weird. I knew I had to take my chances and finally ask David a question that was basically banging the inside of my head.

"David? Who is Victor?"

I waited for a minute for my question to sink in, but it really didn't seem that he would answer me. David released a sigh and ran his hand through his hair.

"I knew I couldn't avoid that question. Alright I'll tell you . . . but I'm going to take you somewhere safe first." David looked away from me and that was the last word he said to me.

I leaned my head against the window I hadn't realized I had a headache, that was a big duh a lump was forming on my head. The cold window helped with easing away some of the pain.

We ended up on a bumpy road a couple of hours later the road pretty much looked like a scene out of a horror movie David pulled over to a complete stop. I couldn't see much because the tree's blocked what little light we had left.

"Where are we?" I turned to David to see him staring at me, I couldn't read what was in his eyes, but he seemed to be a little at ease.

"My home away from home." David replied in a whisper. David parked my car on the side of the road. Come on let's go inside . . . get you cleaned up. I'll answer your questions when we get settled."

"There's a house out there? I can't see it." I squinted my eyes to see if that would help, but still I couldn't see anything.

"Just hold onto me and I'll get us there." David opened the car door and disappeared into the mossy smelling darkness.

David was already on my side of the car. He opened the car door like a gentleman would; it kind of made me smile no guy had ever done that for me—well in my past life chivalry wasn't really dead. His hand was extended towards me; I hesitated but got my bearings back and slipped my hand into his. David's hand was cold but had a hint of warmth that I couldn't describe. My heart began to speed up; I was hoping he couldn't feel my pulse. My memories were back and I could remember everything that happened between us in our past lives together. I managed to get both my feet out of my car and close the door without falling with the help of David of course.

My eye's adjusted to the dim light. In front of me I could just barely make out an entrance gate. David pulled me forward (of course I lost my footing) I stumbled and tripped over a rock. Pain shot up my leg that caused me to gasp. I grabbed my ankle in hoping that I didn't break it.

"I think I twisted my ankle, I'm so freakin elegant sometimes." I felt my face go hot. I couldn't believe I had hurt myself it wasn't even for a good cause.

"I'll carry you don't worry about anything . . . I'm here to help you Anne . . . that's a promise I'm going to keep." David swiped me off the ground like I was a sack of feathers. I wrapped my arms around his neck the closeness was unbelievable. My ankle was still throbbing but being carried by David was keeping my mind off it.

David's black shirt was torn just a little to reveal just a little bit of his shoulder, I could tell that he was built to fight.

"You think you could stand on one foot so that I could open the front gate?" I wasn't paying attention to what he was saying; my eyes were still fixed on the revealed skin of his shoulder.

"Anne . . .

"Hmm . . . oh . . . um what did you say? I was so embarrassed I couldn't even look David in the face.

"Can you stand on one foot for one second so I can open the gate?" I hadn't noticed that we were at the gate already.

"Oh ya I'm fully capable of standing on one foot . . . I don't think I can screw that up."

Obviously I was trying to be funny when I knew very well I wasn't.

David carefully helped place my good foot on the ground slowly so that I wouldn't lose my balance, and fall on my face.

"Hold onto my shoulder." I put my hand on his shoulder my fingers landed on the torn area of his shirt. I tried to pretend that nothing was out of the ordinary. David unlocked the gate I could hear the hinges wine as they were being opened. David picked me up again and walked the rest of the way to the house. We finally made it to the front door he put me down again pulled out a key from his pocket and unlocked the door. David pulled me into his arms again and walked into the house.

The house was so beautiful it was so much better looking than David's house his house had a cold evil presence like someone was watching us. This house had more of a homey feeling there was more of a woman's touch to it.

David sat me in a chair that was in the foyer he locked up the door and turned around to face me.

"Maybe you should take a shower first . . . you know get cleaned up so you can feel better, then we can talk." David was still standing in the hallway.

"That sounds great, but all my stuff is in my car I didn't think of grabbing it."

"Don't worry about that . . . there's a room at the end of the hall help yourself. Just go through the living room theirs a hallway leading up to the rooms."

"Thanks . . . um I'll just take a short shower."

I limped my way through the living room and through the hallway to find a room at the end the door was opened like it was waiting for someone, there were other rooms, but all the doors were closed. I slowly walked through the doorway. The bedroom had a hint of perfume it reminded me of many things. I flicked the switch.

The room was adorned with décor that reminded me of olden day France. There was a dresser displaying many bottles of perfume and makeup. The bed was massive and beautiful the canopy was made of black lace and small black beads. The covers of the bed resembled the color of crimson. I couldn't believe what I was seeing the room was basically something out of my dreams. I limped to the door on the other side of the room I opened the door to find the bathroom I walked in and took in the appearance of the bathroom it had the same color scheme as the room. I walked towards the shower and opened the door it was big enough to fit a group of people I shrugged my shoulders and turned the knob all the way to hot. I unzipped the zippers to my boots and flung them off it was a relief to take them bad boys off.

I basically ripped my clothes off to get into the shower. The hot water was a comfort I stood there to let the water run down my head and face.

My lip stung under the hot water—I took a moment to look over my shoulder the damage had been done-I shook my head and concentrated on the steam gathering around me. I grabbed some shampoo that was near me it smelled like cinnamon, something I would like which was a little strange. I glanced down at my ankle it was developing a fresh bruise. I shook my head and lathered the shampoo into my hair I felt the lump on my head I couldn't believe how many injuries I received in the last couple of days. I ended my shower with a sigh of relief. I hadn't known I was so tired until I saw the bed as I walked out the bathroom. I wrapped myself into a black rope that was hanging behind the door and plopped onto the bed. I could still fell trickles of water running down my body, but I really didn't care.

"Did you find everything to your liking?"

I shot up into an upright position and found David leaning into the doorway.

"Ya . . . um it was great. Did I take too long?

"No not at all . . . I made some food . . . that's if you're hungry. There some clothes in the closet."

"Thanks . . . I'll be out in a minute."

David left me in my new found room. I really didn't know what to do with myself, but I did know I was really hungry. So I decided to find out what was in the closet. I was really hoping it wouldn't be dresses again so I crossed my fingers and held my breath. I yanked open the closet doors to discover every Goth's dream. There was a choice of black and more black and a splash of red in some areas, I never knew anyone who knew me so well. I picked a long sleeved black laced top and a crimson colored top with black lace running along the sides of the shirt. I found pants that screamed 'wear me' there were worn out holes in the knee area, but was covered with see through crimson lace.

I decided to go bare foot I didn't think my ankle would be to happy with me if I wore shoes. I laid everything on the bed and stared at them for a while. Then I realized I needed undergarments. I wondered when David said 'don't worry about it' did he mean he took care of that area to.

I went to the dresser and opened a few drawers. Some of the things in there made me blush. I grabbed a pair of black underwear and a black bra and closed the drawers as fast as possible. Getting dressed was simple enough, but having dinner with David was a whole different matter.

The more I got ready the more I realized I had to confront David. Well I knew avoiding it was not the best idea . . . . plus finding out that he was Alexander and that I was his in the past life was something that made my heart feel oddly warm—I felt like I could ask all the questions in the world that I wanted answers to, but knew I might lack the courage to ask them.

I knew I didn't have to fear David, but I was afraid of the unknown. I mean it's not every day you find out you had a past life with a vampire; who you loved very much and would do anything to be together no matter what, even if it meant death. I knew I couldn't back down now just because I'd bitten off more than I could chew.

The smell of food was distracting me from my thoughts. My stomach growled in such a way that I hoped David couldn't hear it. I couldn't remember if I had any food before all this mess. I guess the smell was my answer to everything. Courage or no courage I had to go.

I walked and partly limped my way through the hallway into the living room and into the kitchen. At home we really didn't use the kitchen anymore, I guess it was only meant to be Mom's job no one could really take her place I knew I couldn't.

"Hey you look different." David was positioned in front of the stove piling a plate with food.

"Um . . . thanks, how did you know what I liked? I nervously shoved my hands into my newly found pants.

"Well I had a little help in that area."

"From who?"

"Well . . . um . . . your Mom often spoke of you and your unusual style . . . these are her words might I add not mine. So I had no trouble at all figuring out what you liked."

I hated the fact that David was able to spend more time with my Mom.

"But how did you know that I would end up here?"

"I'm not too sure Anne . . . I just had a feeling." David grabbed my hand.

"Here come sit down I'm sure you're hungry."

David pulled me into the dining room and placed my plate on the massive dining room table.

"Spaghetti . . . huh . . . well I haven't had that in a while." I limped into the dining room and tried to pull out the chair.

"I'll get that." David positioned me next to him and pulled the chair out for me.

"Thanks . . . I'm not really used to that still."

"Really . . . well I am . . . the very thing you liked about me was that I was such a gentlemen, and amongst many other things."

There was an off settling silence between us, I knew there was so much past history between us, but I really couldn't remember the minor details of our past relationship. Clearly we had stronger feelings for each other I was to scared to open myself to those feelings. The next thing I knew we were sitting across from one another I prayed for courage and broke the silence first.

"Um . . . what did my Mom say about me and my Dad?" David looked up at me.

"What's there to say? She loved you and your Father very much. There wasn't a hateful bone in her body."

"I loved her to . . . I didn't tell her that enough."

"I'm sure she knew . . . I don't think you had to tell her she just knew."

"How do you know that, no one can know that? I should have been a better daughter. I should have done more things for her . . . I should have cleaned my room when she asked me to. Let's just face it I wasn't a daughter a Mother could ask for."

I couldn't help but feel like crap, my Mom was someone I should have loved a little more. I couldn't help but think that I was a pathetic excuse for a daughter.

"How could you say that?" David's eye's turned cold and unreadable.

"Why shouldn't I say it, my Mom loved me and I never appreciated that. Now that she's gone I can't tell her how sorry I am. I blew it no second chances . . . not in this life."

My throat became sore and I couldn't bring myself to say anymore. I lowered my head it was going to be really hard to eat now. I felt tears run down my cheeks I hadn't realized I was crying. I tried brushing the tears away without David noticing.

But David's cool hand made it to my face first. He gently brushed the tears away. I looked up and tried to smile but it was a complete failure.

"You know what's not fair about this Anne? You not knowing how much your Mother loved you, and she knew you loved her too, because every time you visited you never complained."

David grabbed me by the shoulders and lifted me up so that we were eye to eye. "Listen to me Anne, don't you ever think for one minute that you were a horrible daughter to your Mother you weren't and I will swear my life on that."

I wanted more than anything to believe him, but I just couldn't. I let out a sob and buried my face into David's shoulder. "Oh David thanks for trying, but I don't think I'm worth the time and effort."

"You're damned worth everything Anne . . . that's the thing you need to understand. Why do you think I'm here with you right now?

I tried keeping my face hidden in his shoulder, but David managed to pull my face back with the tips of his fingers. We were silent for a while. We were so close to each other my heart began to flutter I kept my eye's lowered to avoid David looking into them.

"Look at me Anne." It was a struggle to not look at him, but I knew I lost. I slowly lifted my eyes. You're a beautiful trustworthy young woman and I've always loved you for that, so there is no way you treated your Mother any differently then I treated mine, and that is saying a lot. So please get those bad thoughts out of your head."

Every word he said to me was spell bounding. David had this power over me and I couldn't understand what it meant.

"Is this your job to? To make people feel better about themselves."

"If it's working . . . then yes it's my job too."

"I'd say it's working David . . . thank you I'm beginning to trust you more than anyone right now."

"I'd say that's a good thing, because right now we only have each other to count on."

It was only then that I realized that I had lost the other five percent of my family. It dawned on me that I was alone for the first time in my life. If David wasn't with me right now I think I would be falling apart.

"I think we're done eating here . . . what do you think Anne?"

"Ya . . . I think so to." I finally got my chance to separate myself from David and do a 180 to the kitchen to clean my dish.

"Hey you don't need to do that you're my guest . . . under the most unusual circumstances, but you're still my guest. Let me get the dishes."

"Okay . . . um thanks." I handed David my plate of half eaten spaghetti and backed away a little so I wouldn't bump into him.

"I'll just go to my room." I left the dining room as fast as possible.

I walked through the hallway and into my room and plopped onto the bed.

I felt so tired and overworked I also hadn't realized that I was sore all over. I plumped up the pillows and rested my head. The coolness of the pillow against my cheek was helpful. My eyes began to droop and finally shut.

You want me to turn you . . . Anne you don't know what you're asking for.

I know what I'm asking for Alexander and that's to spend a very long life with you. There shouldn't even be a shadow of a doubt in your mind Alexander. You either turn me or watch me die a very slow death every day for the rest of your long life.

This is a point in my life that I wish I wasn't a Blue blood only Blue bloods can change others into vampires . . . I didn't want to be put into this position.

You're saying you don't want to turn me?

Look Anne . . . it's hard for me to make a drastic decision like that. Victor doesn't give a damned about you I know if I change you it would only anger him . . . he just wants you out of the picture weather you're a vampire or not.

Why are you avoiding my question Alexander? Do you or do you not want to turn me?

You're asking for something you can't even begin to understand. There is so much to consider here.

The scene changed and a crash emanated right behind Alexander and Anastasia . . .

Victor landed right into the room causing pieces of glass to spray everywhere—Alexander pulled Anastasia closer to him to avoid dangerous pieces of shattered glass from hitting her. Victor turned to face them and glared at them both eyes glowing red.

There is nothing to consider here Alexander . . .

Victor why are you doing this?

Don't you understand Alexander there is no need for someone like her to disrupt the natural order of things. We don't need her . . . turning her is out of the question.

But I love her . . . don't you see . . .

That maybe so, but you are vampire, humans and vampires cannot co-exist together I've told you this many times and yet you still refuse to listen to me! You have left me with no other choice.

Victor reached into his jacket and pulled out a menacing looking knife.

What are you doing Victor?

Something that should have been done a long time ago Alexander. Victor jumped at Alexander and threw him across the room leaving Anastasia venerable.

Nooooooo!

I was trying to get myself out of my nightmare trying to scratch and hit anything that came my way.

"Anne hold on . . . stop trying to scratch me! Open your eyes! It's me David!"

I hadn't realized that the one I was trying scratch was David, I felt so embarrassed.

"I—I'm so sorry . . . I didn't mean . . .

"Shhh its okay you were having a bad dream Anne." David was holding me by the arms.

"How bad was the dream Anne?"

"That's the thing David it's not dreams it my memories coming back to me it was like I was back there again . . . I could actually feel the knife . . . I couldn't help it I started crying. David pulled me into his arms and pushed my hair away from my face.

"I know it's really hard for you . . . but you don't need to hold it in Anne . . . just talk to me. This is why we are here . . . for you to talk and ask questions, and I'll answer them the best way I can."

It felt good to be close to someone and for a moment I didn't want to be anywhere else but here, but two question lingered in my mind.

"What do I do David? Where do I go from here?"

We sat there on the bed I didn't want him to let go of me I felt so safe with him. All these things I was experiencing in my memories were really getting to me.

"I don't know what to tell you, but what I can do is help you through all of this and keep you safe, because I'll be damned if Victor gets you again. I will not go through the loss of you again."

"Can I ask my questions now?" I kept my face buried in David's chest so it came out muffled, but I was sure he understood me.

"Yes you may Anne ask away."

"Who is Victor I can't really gather who he is in my memories . . . what does he want with me . . . and why does . . . . ." I guess I had more questions than I thought because they were pouring out of me.

"Hold on that's more than one question Anne . . . take a breath and ask one question at a time."

"Okay let's go with the first question. Who is he?" David pulled away from me and sat at the furthest part of the bed.

"All right but you're not going to like it very much . . . I didn't even have the courage to tell you in our past life . . . I was going to, but he got to you before I could tell you."

I could tell this was going to be very hard for him—there was a shadow over his eyes and somehow that made him look darker than usual.

David sighed and turned to look at me. "Victor is my brother." David stopped to see my initial reaction.

"What you're kidding me right?!" I was in shock. "What brother would want to destroy your life like that?"

"Unfortunately . . . I'm not kidding." David lowered his eyes and for a moment I thought he might cry. I moved closer to him and placed my hand on his shoulder.

"Why David—why did he do this to you?"

"Because he had plans for me Anne and you came into my life . . ."

"So I messed up Victor's plans?"

"No Anne you didn't . . . I was happy with you, and I thought Victor would be happy with you to, but he wasn't . . . he hated the idea that I was with you."

"What was so wrong with me?"

"There was absolutely nothing wrong with you Anne . . . I loved you . . . but he couldn't get past the fact that you were human then and he still can't get over it now."

"So what was wrong with the idea of turning me . . . that would have fixed everything right?"

"No . . . he didn't want me to turn anyone . . . he told me it would have upset the balance of things . . . Victor couldn't have a newborn . . . . he said it would have been difficult."

"Why would it be difficult?" I slipped my hand into David's.

"Because me and Victor are Blue Blood's we've lived for a long time and have succumbed to many things a newborn can't."

"So if you changed me what would happen?" David looked up at me his eye's looked so sad.

"You would live a very difficult life Anne . . . you will never live by day and the hunger you will have will be stronger than anything you've ever felt . . . . this is why Victor will not allow me to change you the risk is too high.

"So you won't change me?"

"No I won't . . . . I don't really know if I could do such a thing to you."

Yes it would have been very difficult to make this decision, my past self wanted it more then anything, but my present self couldn't decide . . . to never live by day would be torture . . . what would I do if I couldn't see my Dad again or my friends . . . . it would be a very difficult decision.

"Anne . . .

"David placed his hand on my shoulder.

"Yes David?"

"You have to really think about this . . . rushing to make a decision is very dangerous . . . there are things you would have to do as a newborn . . .

"What would that be?" I got really nervous I didn't know what he was going to tell me.

"The hunt . . . ." David looked away from me.

"What is it David?"

"You would have to hunt for humans . . . there's nothing else you can do Anne."

"No way . . . . I can't do that David!"

"Then the decision is easier for you Anne."

"Do you hunt for . . .

"No Anne I don't . . . . not anymore I've not needed to hunt . . . let's not talk about this Anne.

"Alright fine . . . . so what happened to us after Victor disapproved.

"We were going to runaway together."

"But Victor got to us before we could leave . . . and that's when I died."

"Anne he killed you because he couldn't get his way."

"But he didn't plan for me to be reincarnated, and he didn't plan for me to get parts of my memory back . . . I guess god does exist."

"I didn't expect that to happen either . . . when you died . . . my life after that was hell . . . I took your body and mourned for several years I had you buried at a place that we both loved . . . Your favorite flowers grew in that very spot." But when I left France I had you moved. Throughout the years I always had a team of people help me move you wherever I went. When I settled here in Ravendell I had you moved to Hill cemetery.

"And that's how I bumped into you at the cemetery, you were visiting my grave, chills went down my spine the idea of it was crazy. "So you were going to put that black rose in your jacket pocket on my grave?

"Yes I was . . . I forgot it was in there when I bumped into you . . . when you found it the look on your face was recognition . . . I knew you knew something about it.

"Yes I did David it was at that point I saw the black rose in my dreams it was at that point that I thought they were dreams . . . but when I saw that flower I knew something was familiar about it, but I couldn't tell you." I looked up at David he was looking at me so intensely. I looked back down and moved to another question.

"So what did you do after all of this?" I couldn't stop asking questions—I wanted to know every detail of his life after me.

"Well after you died I wanted to dedicate myself in helping others—Victor didn't understand why, but there was no way I was ever going to let him get in between me and whatever it was I had to do—I hated him so much."

"So you became a Doctor and that's what you have been doing ever since?"

"Yes pretty much." My eyes were feeling heavy again we finally ended up lying down on the bed—me asking questions and him answering them as best as he could.

Sun Rise

I woke up in a hue of pinkish light I was the only one occupying the bed. I felt safe to know that I had fallen asleep while David was lying right next to me. With a sigh and a long awaited stretch I got up from the bed and walked up to the window. The blinds were shut I stuck my finger on one of the flaps and pulled down. There was nothing to be seen, but the sky and the pinkish light peeking through the branches of the woods. I didn't hear any birds chirping or see any animals crawling around. With that I decided to explore the house for a while maybe see what life David had made for himself out here in the woods. The door to my room was still opened I was expecting to hear some sort of noises coming from the front of the house, but there was nothing.

I walked through the hallway—there was nothing—no one, it felt really strange and frightening at the same time. I wanted to call out Davids' name, but I thought better of it. My heart was thumping around my chest and I knew it wasn't going to stop. I was still standing in the same spot in the hallway I decided to limp back to my room I closed the door behind me and sat in a chair that was near me. My bags were right next to the chair leg I guess David brought them in for me once I passed out then it hit me I hadn't checked my phone for two days. I could imagine the messages that were left on it. I popped my fingers took a deep breath and exhaled I grabbed my phone out of my bag with shaking hands sure enough the light to my phone was flashing red to indicate that I had unheard and unread text messages. I flipped my phone opened I wasn't sure if I wanted to hear the yelling or read the angry text messages, but I felt like I needed to get it over with.

Twelve voice messages were waiting to be heard I decided there was no point to delay it any longer I placed the phone to my ear and waited for the first angry voice.

Message 1 Tammy

"Anne it's me Tammy can you please call me back I didn't mean to say those things . . . You know I'm just trying to help . . . can't you see that?"

Message 2 Dad

"Hey Anne its Dad . . . Running away from home isn't the best answer come back home and we can sort out everything together honey.

Message 3 Tammy

"Okay Anne seriously your starting to freak me out . . . you never forget to call me . . . is there any possible way you can call your best friend back . . . you know just for good measure . . . PLEASE!"

Message 4 Dad

"Alright Anne Tammy won't stop calling the house . . . she's becoming worried and so am I . . . Don't do this to me Anne I'm doing my best to be a good Father and I would like for you to acknowledge that . . . PLEASE GIVE ME A CALL AS SOON AS YOU CAN!"

I knew if I continued to listen to the messages they were going to get a lot worse—Dad was never good at being composed—let alone understanding.

Message 5 Dad

"ALRIGHT ANNE I'M GOING OUT TO FIND YOU . . . I DON'T KNOW WHERE I'M GOING TO START, BUT FOR NOW THE CEMETARY IS MY BEST GUESS! YOU'RE

MAKING THIS REALLY HARD FOR ME AND I REALLY DON'T KNOW WHY! THIS IS YOUR LAST CHANCE TO CALL ME AND TELL ME YOUR OKAY . . . AND PLEASE FIND YOUR WAY HOME . . . I DON'T KNOW WHAT TO THINK ANYMORE . . . I CAN'T LOSE YOU EITHER . . . COME HOME PLEASE!"

Message 6 Dad

"WHERE ARE YOU ANNE . . . I HAVE BEEN UP THE WALL . . . WORRIED AS HELL . . . I'VE CALLED EVERYONE YOU KNOW AND NO ONE SEEMS TO KNOW WHERE YOU ARE! I'VE GONE TO THE CEMETARY! I'M YOUR FATHER I HAVE EVERY RIGHT TO BE CONCERNED I WOULD HAVE NEVER THOUGHT YOU WOULD EVER PULL A STUNT LIKE THIS! I WANT TO KNOW WHERE YOU ARE AND I WANT YOU HOME RIGHT NOW NO IF AND'S OR BUT'S ABOUT IT ANNE . . ."

Message 7 Tyler

"You know it figures that you would run away from your problems . . . . I never expected you to be such a coward. But you know what I'm going to do—I'm going to come and find you Anne."

I didn't know what scared me more Dads' phone messages or Tyler's calm and collected message.

You can pretty much guess what the other eighteen hundred text messages were about. The tears would not stop and I had no idea what to do . . . . I felt like I did the right thing—heck I know I did the right thing all I was doing was protecting the only family I had left—ya calling would probably be a good idea, but I didn't think I would have the strength to handle all the anger. I knew exactly what I needed and that was Davids' advice and maybe his embrace, but the question was where was he exactly.

I finally gathered up the strength to get myself off the chair and half ran half limped through the hallway and into the living room. I stopped in the middle of the living room and did a 180 to the kitchen.

"David where are you . . . I need you!" There wasn't an answer back.

"Please I need to talk to you . . . please I need you David!"

There was another hallway I hadn't noticed it before it was at the farthest part of the kitchen. If David around he must have a room, and my best guess was that it was down this hallway.

"David . . ." I said his name in a hush tone that I wasn't even sure I heard myself say it.

Slowly I walked my way through the hallway. There was an old looking elevator at the end of it I was surprised I had never seen an elevator in a house before. There was a small button on the wall next to the elevator . . . . with a shacking hand I managed to press the button. I was sure I was going to hear the corny bell, but there wasn't. I hesitated and managed to take a glance behind me it didn't seem like anything was out of the ordinary. Stepping through the elevator was easy, but not knowing my destination was harder I hadn't really thought this through, but it was way to late the doors closed, and I could feel the elevator descend. My lungs were starting to feel tight and I thought I might hyperventilate.

The elevator halted and paused for just a moment the doors opened slowly. This was a bad idea and I knew it, but I felt like I couldn't turn back now. So I walked out of the elevator and into a hallway.

Dim lights were lining the ceiling above me—it was somewhat of a comfort. There was a faint scent like a perfume it almost smelled like roses, but I wasn't too sure. There was an opening at the end of the hallway leading into what looked like a bedroom. I bit my lip in hoping I wasn't going somewhere I wasn't supposed to be. I turned the corner and stopped in my footsteps. Their laying in a very large bed was David he seemed so motionless like he could be dead (well officially). I think I gasped but I couldn't tell I must have because David moved—I leaped back into the hallway I wanted to run like hell, but I froze and couldn't move.

"Anne?" David's voice was so husky it made my heart speed up. "I can hear you Anne there's no need for you to hide."

When I said I was biting my lip before I was basically cutting into my lip now. I slumped my shoulders and came out from my hiding spot.

"I didn't mean to . . . I tired . . . um well . . . I couldn't bring myself to say anything the words didn't seem to be there. David was just sitting there the blanket fell from him I could just see his strong chest in the dim light. He seemed to be carved out of stone.

"It's okay Anne quit your stammering and tell me what happened . . . your face is completely streaked with tears." I had forgotten that I was crying just a moment ago, I tried wiping away the evidence, but I felt it was hopeless.

"My Dad is ready to have a heart attack, because he can't find me and my friends are freaking out well just one of them, Tyler is threatening to come and find me . . . I want to call all of them, but I don't think that's the best idea—plus I don't even know what to tell them—I don't think they would believe me." I sat at the edge of the bed and crossed my arms across my chest.

"What do I do David—What can I do to fix this?!" Yelling seemed to be the best thing I could do at the moment. I covered my face with both my hands and began to cry David immediately got up and pulled me into his arms.

"I think maybe that's something we need to handle together at a later date. Maybe it's safe for all of them to not to know what's going on at the moment. The less they know the better it will be."

I could feel David's breath on the top of my head as he was talking—it calmed me for a moment.

"If you can't help me . . . does that mean I have to stay away forever . . . to keep my Dad safe . . . I mean I want everyone to be safe.

There was an unknown silence between us. "I don't know what will transpire, but I do know we have to take this slowly." The only thing I could do was sigh and take it all in. David wrapped his arms around me and held me there. My heart kept telling me that this was where I was supposed to be.

"Just tell me . . . is everything going to be okay? I don't care if you lie to me . . . just tell me anything I don't care."

I looked up at him, but he wasn't looking at me. David was looking above my head at an unknown source.

"You don't have to worry Anne I'll do anything . . . even if that means killing someone."

The thought of David killing someone was a bit shocking—could he do it on account of me and my family? I had no doubt about it.

"I think maybe I should go back to my room now David . . . sorry I bothered you." I pushed myself away from him.

"You may go . . . but I must stay here." David lowered his eyes—he didn't seem to be sad, but determined.

"Why?" There was space in between us but very little.

"Because my feelings for you are very overwhelming." David filled the void that was in between us—I started shaking a little—David gently brushed his index finger along my jaw line.

"Ugh . . . well . . ." my breathing became very shallow I was trying to back away, and found myself against the wall. There was nowhere to go but forward. "I'll leave . . ."

"Ssshhh its okay Anne." David's eye's were glowing again—I couldn't get over how green they were.

My eyes fell on his lips I could just see the tips of his fangs—for some reason it didn't frighten me.

"Do you know what it was like living without you Anne? David pulled me into his arms, and his hand lowered to the small of my back I could feel his hand brush along the skin that was revealed. I gasped a little. I wanted to be with David I could feel it in my heart—I had no idea where it was coming from maybe it was Anastasias' feelings that were coming through my own—I knew that I didn't want him to stop.

"No . . . I'm sorry I don't." Davids' head lowered just below my chin my heart started to thump really fast again. David pulled me closer to his body my hand landed on his bare chest. I could feel my body heat swarm into him. He did the most unbelievable thing he kissed my neck in a slow wanting need. A gasp escaped my lips and that was all it took.

Our lips finally met and we couldn't stop. The smell of roses got even stronger as he pulled my legs around his waist. David carried me back to his bed and gently lowered my body onto the soft mattress. Every muscle on David's back was firm I couldn't stop my hands from exploring every curve of his back. David's lips were so soft I couldn't bring my mind to compare it to anything. David pulled away from me and looked straight into my eyes.

"I guess you missed me?" I said innocently.

"You better believe it Anne." He kissed me again sending chills down my spine. I could feel his hands slip behind my back. My kisses became more urgent I wanted more which scared me.

I thought I would be lost in this moment forever until my cell phone decided to ring.

After the second ring I was standing upright and David was across the room putting on his shirt.

"You shouldn't answer that Anne." David said huskily

I grabbed my phone out of my back pocket and looked at the screen unfortunately it was Dad I pressed the talk button on the fourth ring . . . . I couldn't ignore it anymore.

"Hey Dad . . . .

"Anne what have you gotten yourself into?" Dad's voice sounded unsteady.

"What do you mean Dad?" I couldn't imagine what my Dad knew.

"Anne darling where are you . . . theirs a man here who wants . . . .

I could feel the blood rush to my head . . . "David . . .

David came from his side of the room and grabbed me by the shoulders. "What is it Anne . . . what's wrong?"

"David . . . he has my Dad . . . .

Confrontation

"Good now that I have your attention." I could feel his stupid hot breath through my cell phone I didn't think that was possible. I could tell Victor was pleased with himself he was really beginning to pissing me off, but I was scared at the same time, because I knew he had my Dad and there was no telling what he was doing to him.

"Please don't hurt my Dad!" It was all too much I couldn't even think straight.

"Oh I haven't hurt him, but I think he got the message."

"I HATE YOU VICTOR!" Before I knew it David snatched my phone out of my hand and put it to he's ear. Something was being said to David it was killing me inside not to know what it was . . . . my Dad's life was at stake and I had no idea what to do about it. I was snapped out of my thoughts when David finally said something.

"Alright we'll stay put . . . . no we won't go anywhere . . . . just bring her Dad over here unharmed . . . YES VICTOR UNHARMED! DO YOU HEAR ME UNHARMED! David slammed my phone onto a dresser nearby.

"What are we going to do David?" I could feel my heart beating one hundred miles per hour I was beginning to feel lightheaded, next thing I knew I was hyperventilating. Between my gasps I uttered . . . "I don't . . . . think I can . . . handle this!" I fell to my knees I could just picture what was happening to my Dad.

David grabbed me and guided me to the elevator. "How did I get my Dad into this?"

"You didn't." David wouldn't look at me.

"And why not . . . how isn't it my fault?

"Because you can't blame yourself for something that happened in the past, and because I should have stayed away I brought this on you and your Father."

David pulled me into the elevator and the doors closed behind us. "I'm going to fix this Anne . . . I'm going to get your Father out of this."

The elevator doors slowly opened David grabbed me by the arm and with lightening speed ran through the hallway, and into the living room.

I could barley speak with all the emotion I was feeling.

"This won't end until I'm dead . . . . right?"

David grabbed me by my arm and pulled me behind him. "What are you doing David?"

"Exactly right little Anne." I nearly cursed when I heard Victors voice.

"Don't you dare touch my daughter!" I peeked over David's shoulder to see my Dad on the floor tied up I gasped because I had never seen my Dad so venerable in my entire life. Next to my Dad were Tammy and Tyler they weren't moving at all.

"Anne it seems I have kept my end of the bargain your dear old Dad is unharmed as I promised, but I ran into a problem seems your friends wanted to join the bargain to. Victor was smiling I couldn't understand how Victor could be such a monster.

"Your Dad can stay unharmed if you don't do anything foolish, but I can't really say that for your friends."

"Please! What did you do to my friends!" I couldn't stop crying.

"You can't have her Victor." David looked like he was ready to do something foolish.

"Oh really well I think we can come to some sort of an arrangement."

"No don't hurt my daughter!"

"Ugh you humans are always so rude." I could tell Victor was getting really annoyed.

"WHAT THE HELL ARE YOU TALKING ABOUT . . . UNTIE ME RIGHT NOW!!"

I was praying to god for Dad to stop yelling I knew Victor wouldn't take it.

"WHO ARE YOU TO GIVE ME ORDERS!? Next thing I knew Victor grabbed my Dad and threw him through the nearest wall. I couldn't believe it.

"NNNOOOO!!!!" I tried to geting around David, but he wouldn't let me.

"YOU PROMISED VICTOR . . . LET ME GO DAVID!" The wall was completely destroyed I couldn't tell what was my Dad and what wasn't my Dad. My heart was breaking.

"I'm a vampire not a saint little Anne." The smile on Victor's face was menacing I knew then that he didn't care about a damned thing.

"DON'T CALL ME THAT!"

"Ooohhh someone's getting a little angry . . . no matter that doesn't change a thing. Well David I hope you don't mind I decided to bring some friends along."

David grabbed me by the shoulders. "Anne I really need you to do something for me."

"What do you need me to do David?"

"I need you to run . . . ."

"But my Dad he needs me, and my friends." From where I was standing I hadn't seen my Dad move at all I really didn't want to think the worse. Tammy and Tyler still hadn't moved one inch.

"You can't help them right now it's hopeless . . . now more than ever I want you to listen to me."

"What are you two whispering to each other over there? Marcus! Gabrielle! Come on out and separate these two!"

"Now would be a good idea to listen to me Anne. Run and don't you dare try anything!

David pushed me toward the direction of the front door of course I tripped all over my feet.

"Marcus! Don't you dare let her get away! I turned around to see David struggling to keep Victor, Marcus, and Gabrielle away from me it was amazing I stopped to look at the intensity of the fight, and then it hit I was speechless—the two men my Dad trusted to bring in his home weren't Detectives at all they were in league with Victor this whole time.

"DAMMIT ANNE RUUUNNN!

I snapped out of it and ran to the front door and fumbled with the door knob I tried to yank it open, but it wouldn't. 'Oh shit!' was the only thing that was going through my mind at that very moment. David was struggling to keep all three men away from me. "IT WON'T OPEN!!

"BREAK THE DAMNED WINDOW I DON'T CARE JUST GET THE HELL OUT OF HERE ANNE!"

I turned around to see David throw Marcus across the room he smacked his head on a nearby post if he had been a human that would have knocked him out cold, but I wasn't dealing with anything human.

I looked around to see if there was anything to break the window with and low and behold I was in luck, I grabbed a big huge statue of a bird and threw it at the window. It worked.

I swiped away the glass from the ledge I put one leg out of the window—I thought I was home free, but someone grabbed my other leg. I freaked and turned around to see Gabrielle's fangs out.

Before I knew it David pushed Gabrielle across the room causing him to crash through the living room wall. "I can't hold them off forever Anne go now!"

I grabbed the panel of the window, but my clammy hand slipped and I ended up falling out of the window and landing on my back. A burning sensation on my right leg made me realize that I cut myself on the glass. I finally got myself up off the ground my bare feet were covered in so much mud.

There were so many thoughts running through my head I was so worried about my Dad and my friends. I didn't want them to die.

I could hear more crashing sounds and growling. I looked around and decided that my best bet would have to be the forest. My leg was hurting like hell, but I knew I had to put that out of my mind. I ran a few paces towards the gate, but as I got closer to the gate I heard a crashing noise I turned to see the front door flying towards me I screamed and ducked out of the way. I looked up to see David lying on the ground and Victor walking through the door way.

"Well hello Anne I didn't think David would fight so well for you, but it seems he's grown weak over 'the past years' shall we say." Victor was standing next to David's unmoving body, and I could just see Marcus and Gabrielle standing behind him.

"So let's give up this whole charade shall we, and just come with me Anne." Victor was smiling, but his smile had something hidden behind it like a wanting to take something apart, but it sure as hell wasn't going to be me.

"Oh hell no I'm not going anywhere with you!" I didn't hesitate one bit I ran for it.

The River

I ran for who knows how long, but when I stopped I knew I was lost. I was breathing so hard that my chest began to hurt. All my life I never knew I would be in this situation. The worst thing that's happened to me was losing someone I loved, but never running for my life . . . . from angry vampires. I could hear Victor's angry voice a couple of meters back I knew I had to continue running, but I didn't know where. I could tell there was a river, everything was so green I knew if I could get across that river I just might have a chance of making it. My side was aching in pain, but I knew I had to keep going I could feel blood running down my leg I knew I could be easily found by my blood alone. David was nowhere to be seen I was worried for him I wanted to stay and help him, but I knew very well I couldn't. I stopped and listened—the sound of rushing water made my heart beat faster I ran through the brush and tress I had scratches all over my arms and I could feel a stinging sensation on my face. I finally found the edge of the forest and in front of me was the river.

I ran up to the edged of the water and stuck my leg in it was so frigid my teeth slammed together I had no idea what I was doing, but fending for my life would make me do anything stupid. It was so dark in the forest I couldn't even see my own outstretched hand. The water was rushing past my feet it was a fast current I was praying to god I would make it across. I had no fear of water, but I did here a lot of stories about drowning victims, and they all ended tragically. The snapping of a stick distracted me from the task at hand. I turned around to find someone standing there 'David' I thought at first, but he wasn't so tall. I knew who it was . . . I had no time to react. I wanted to scream and shout, but it was too late. Victor rammed right into me and we were both sent into the rushing current of the river. I lost all hope in being able to live through this day.

My lungs were screaming for air, I knew Victor lost me when we fell into the river I finally surfaced and breathed in a wonderful gulp of air, but as I was doing this I was rammed from the side and grabbed by strong arms.

"David can't save you now Anne you will die like you did so many centuries ago, and now you're going to die today." I had no fight left in me anymore and I knew if I tried struggling I was only going to die a lot faster.

Victor rammed into me and dragged me all the way down to the bottom of the river. I didn't want to die like this, but tugging at Victor was like trying to tug a stone off of me. I tried holding my breath in, but as much as I tried Victor banged my back onto a nearby rock the breath was knocked right out of me, all the water rushed into my mouth and lungs. It hurt I hadn't imagine drowning would be so painful. This was it, this was how I was going to die I was growing weak and I knew my body was giving up on me. My vision became fuzzy everything turned to white I felt myself being pulled up by some sort of force that was unexplainable I didn't feel myself fight it maybe I was floating back up to the surface maybe I wasn't going to die.

I opened my eyes to find myself lying in a room that was completely white. There was this brightness that I couldn't really understand I sat up and took a look at myself; what I saw was unbelievable—I had visions of myself as Anastasia, but as I looked at myself I was her I felt black silk touch my face or so that's what I thought it was . . . my hair was really long and the dress I was wearing was made of dark blue satin. I got up from the floor my leg wasn't hurting anymore I lifted up my dress and looked at my right leg it wasn't bleeding, and there were no sign of a wound. This was starting to get really weird I took both my hands and rubbed them against my eyes.

"Anne?" I stopped rubbing my eyes and kept them there for a moment, because I wasn't to sure what I just heard and from whom I heard it from. My hands were pulled away from my eyes and I couldn't believe who was standing right in front of me.

Not My Time

"Mom?" I couldn't believe it; she was here standing in front of me.

"Yes darling it's me." I pulled my arms out of her grasp and backed away to the nearest wall.

"Don't be scared Anne it's just me . . . . it's Mom."

"But . . . . this can't . . . . be possible. Where am I?" I couldn't believe what was happening; she was just standing there like this was normal—like nothing had happened to her. She was exactly how I remembered her when I was a child—beautiful long black hair and blue eyes that had so much life in them.

"Well it's me Anne, and it seems my dear Anne that you are passing on."

"What!!!! I nearly fell.

"I know hard to believe . . . . but here you are. Come sit with me." She held her hand out I hesitated a little—She grabbed my hand and brought me towards some chairs that I swore weren't there before. We sat down next to each other and stared at one another for a while.

"So I'm . . . . dead?" It was hard to even let those words go pass my lips.

"Oh honey in a way you are."

"In a way I am? What's that supposed to mean?" Well as if I weren't confused already—now I'm even more confused. What the hell am I supposed to do with that?

"Well Hun this is the meeting point for everyone who is just about to pass on to the other side."

"So my fate is decided . . . I have to die again and lose loving David in the process, and what about Dad, and my friends?"

"No . . . . not this time Anne and there's not much I can say about the fate of your Father and your friends." Mom was looking at me with such intensity that it kind of threw me off when she said "no" and my heart sank for Dad, Tammy and Tyler. My thoughts returned to my outcome.

"What do you mean not this time?"

"You—my daughter have suffered in the lives before you and in your life now. It has seemed that you will not go through this again. Anne you have more to accomplish with your life, then you know."

"But how would you know what I've gone through . . . I mean in the past?"

"It shouldn't matter how I know. What matters now is that we get you back where you belong."

All of what Mom was saying overwhelmed me—was I going to get a second chance with David?

"It's time to go Anne." I looked up to see my Mom staring at me, she had this knowing in her eyes like there was more to this then what she was telling me.

"Ohhhhhh! Mom I've missed you, and now I have to lose you again!"

I grabbed her and hugged her in such a way that I thought maybe I didn't want to go back, that maybe I truly was meant to be dead, but I loved David I couldn't imagine hurting him again.

"No Anne . . . you never lost me I've always been their . . . in your mind . . . in your heart . . . and right now your going to be strong and go back.

"But . . . .

All of a sudden I felt this sting on my neck . . . It felt like my whole entire left side of my neck was on fire.

"MOM! SOMETHINGS WRONG!" My legs buckled, my arms were still warped around my Mom's shoulders.

"Shhhhh Anne its okay . . . just breath . . . do this for me Anne."

I could feel my body being lowered—everything started to go fuzzy again.

"Breath Anne just breath." The echo of my Mom's voice was the worst part of this whole experience. I wanted to cry.

"Mom!" I could feel something pining me down to the ground, and the pain was unbearable.

I opened my eyes to find Victor on top of me.

"No please stop don't do this! I struggled to get him off of me.

Victor stopped and pulled his mouth away from my neck. "Wait you were dead!"

"I'm meant to live Victor . . . I'll keep fighting to live!"

Victor's mood changed from being pretty damned hungry to pretty pissed off.

"Well then I'm just going to have keep killing you! Until you give up on wanting to live!

"No ill keep fighting you I refuse to let you win Victor . . .

I was interrupted by the sound of David's beautiful voice.

"Get away from her Victor I'm warning you! Victor snarled and was about to sink his teeth back into my neck.

"No!!"

David rammed right into Victor amazingly not hitting me in the process. I positioned myself into a ball and covered my face with my hands. I could hear the growling and a terrible crunch. I winced in part because my neck was hurting like hell, and because I couldn't tell who just got the wrong end of the stick.

"David . . . ." I was scared and in a lot of pain, there was something really wrong with me. My body was trembling and I felt really hot my eyes wear shut to the point where I didn't think I could open them. Something grabbed me and lifted me up from the ground.

"Anne are you okay?" I managed to open my eyes to find David looking at me in concern.

"Oh David you're okay!!!!" I flung my arms around his neck I completely forgetting everything I was going through.

"Yes Anne I'm okay." David wrapped his arms around my waist and pulled me closer.

"I died David." He tried to pull away from me, but I clung to him so he wouldn't be able to look into my eyes. "Please let me get this off my chest. "I died and I saw my Mom . . . .

I placed my cheek on his shoulder and closed my eyes. The pain was still there, but I was fighting it to get my words out. David was quite.

"She was beautiful . . . . like the way she was before she got sick. She told me I was meant to live, but I got this really weird feeling like she was keeping something from me.

"I don't think I could have been able to lose you again Anne" . . . David pulled my face up and kissed me lightly on the forehead.

"I know David—so what do I do now? . . . . I mean can I stop running? Is Victor dead?" I tried to look around to see if I could spot Victor, but David grabbed my face with both his hands.

"I think that's a bad idea—I think with your current state right now . . . you don't need to see what I did to him." That worried me to the point that I started to shake—I felt like it was my fault for everything that had happened. My mind couldn't wrap around what David might have done to Victor. Would this change him? As my thoughts swirled around in my mind a vision of my Dad and my friend's pushed all those thoughts to the back of my mind.

"I think it's time to get out of here."

"David . . . ."

"What is it Anne?"

"My Dad . . . . my friends."

Alone

My heart was pounding in my ears as I tried to make my way out of the forest. I kept tripping over fallen branches and loose rocks. The cut on my leg was bothering me like hell, but I knew I needed to get to my Dad and my friends—Dad was hurt for sure, but I didn't know what was wrong with Tammy and Tyler, but what I didn't want to do was bring myself into thinking something much worse than that.

David was walking right next to me trying to keep an even pace with a human like me.

We finally found ourselves at the opening of the forest through the opened gate I could see David's house it looked like a war zone, the whole front of David's house was torn apart the front door was completely gone, I knew that because it barely missed my head as I was running away. I kept getting a really bad feeling like this day wasn't going to end so well not like it was going well for that matter. What was worse about this whole thing was that my body was in so much pain that I couldn't breathe most of the time.

"You okay Anne?" David placed his hand on my shoulder.

"I'm fine." I started to run towards the house I kept expecting to see my Dad, Tyler and Tammy waiting for me, with worried expressions on their face's and the gladness to see that I was okay, but they weren't waiting for me they were nowhere to be seen. I grew even more scared as I ran into the house and through the living room Tammy and Tyler were still lying where Victor had left them they hadn't moved at all. I ran to the very spot where my Dad's body was thrown.

There he was laying their body crumbled in such a way I never thought was possible. I could tell that there was no life in my Dad. I knelt down, and placed my hand on my Dad's chest I couldn't feel his heart beating.

"No . . . No . . . Oh Dad!!!!" I lifted him into my arms—his head was all bloody and bruised.

I pulled my Dad closer to me—and all the emotion I held back in the past, and even now came out into the most heart wrenching scream. Tears were pouring out of my eyes nonstop my heart was being ripped in two. I had lost the only link to a normal life and my best friends were either dead or just badly hurt.

"Anne?"

"What David!" I was rocking back and forth with my Dad in my arms.

"We have to go." I could hear the emotion in his voice.

"I can't leave him here David." I sniffled

"I know Anne, but we can't stay here much longer, I got rid of both Marcus and Gabrielle, but we don't have much time."

"It's easy for you isn't it! Not having" . . . . the pain came back again only much worse this time.

"Uggghhh . . . David there's something wrong!" My stomach felt like it was on fire, I put my hand against my stomach, but that did nothing.

"What's wrong Anne?!" David knelt down right next to me.

"Something's not right!" Another stabbing pain went through my stomach—I fell to the ground screaming in pain not only that, but a stinging sensation started to rip through my neck.

"David please help me!!!!" I was curled up into a ball trying not to vomit. The pain was unbearable—I put my hand on my neck to try to stop the pain, but it wasn't working at all nothing was. It was then I realized I was never ever going to experience anything human ever again.

"What is it Anne—what's hurting you?!!! David grabbed me and pulled me into his arms.

"Victor . . . My breathing was becoming more labored.

"What about him Anne?! What did he do to you?!" David was beginning to panic now.

"Victor . . . bit me! On those last words I screamed in agony—my back was arched, and I was digging my finger nails into my palms.

"Nnooooo . . . Anne—This can't be happening!!"

I could feel myself changing I was shivering I couldn't breathe. My mind was swimming with memories—my heart speed fast as I saw my current life flash before my eyes it caused me pain like nothing I'd ever felt before I didn't understand why god chose to show me, but he did and it broke my heart; as time went by I finally felt my body go still everything went blank in my mind.

"Anne please . . . wake up." I could hear the mournful agony in David's voice. I opened my eyes, everything seemed so vivid—it was blurry at first, but everything became clearer as I blinked my eyes. David was still holding me in his arms. I felt so much different—and there was no more pain. I turned my head and David was looking right at me.

"I'm a . . . .

"I'm so sorry Anne I didn't know he bit you . . . this should have never happened to you Anne I didn't want your life to be ended in such a way. My dear sweat Anne he turned you."

I took a look at myself in a nearby mirror . . . . my hair had grown past my waist and my skin looked so pale—I looked closer my eyes appeared to almost be black. I shook my head and looked back at David.

"So then . . . I can never go back to being . . .

"No . . . I'm so sorry Anne." Tears were coming from his eyes.

"It's not your fault David." I placed my hand on his cheek and brushed away his tears.

"It is my fault Anne and I will never forgive myself." David pulled me into his arms and hugged me in such a way that made me feel so sad.

"I can't be selfish anymore David . . . . I lost two very important people in my life, and I'm not even sure if my friends are alive I felt so alone even more now, but I know one thing David."

"And what's that?" David mumbled into my neck.

"I have you and now you have me . . . . we have to stick together now." David pulled away and looked into my eyes.

"If that's what you want Anne."

"Yes David that's what I want—that's all I ever wanted."

David looked into my eyes—as if to see what was truly in them. "Then we have to go Anne." He pulled me up.

"What about my Dad and my friends?" Dad was laying their flat on his back—Tyler and Tammy were still lying unmoving on the floor.

"My Dad never deserved to die like this." I stared at my Dads face . . . he looked so pale. David went to him and picked him up with such ease, as if he weighed nothing at all.

"Your Father will have a proper burial—I won't have it any other way." I felt the tears come and they flowed over just as well as if I were still a human.

"And I will see if your friends are okay." David put my Dad on the couch, and walked towards my friends. First he went to Tyler; David checked his pulse and then went to Tammy and checked her's. I stood up and crossed my arms I didn't know what David was going to tell me, I was afraid that I lost them to. David walked up to me and looked at me his eyes were unreadable.

"Their alive Anne . . . . I was relieved that they were alive, but I didn't like the way David turned around, and looked at both my friends.

"So why aren't they responding David?" He turned around to face me.

"It seems that both of them are . . . . in a state of coma." I looked at my friends and then looked back at David.

"You're not serious . . . . that's not true it can't be!" I ran to Tyler and grabbed him into my arms.

"Please wake up Tyler don't do this to me . . . . I need you!" Tyler didn't respond. Tears flowed out of my eyes and blurred my vision. I went to Tammy and grabbed her into my arms.

"You can't do this Tammy you have to wake up . . . there's so many things you can't miss . . . please wake up!" A sob escaped my lips.

"David please help them . . . . do something anything!" I ran up to David looking him straight in his eyes.

"I cannot—they need to go to the hospital."

"So then what happens to them?"

"They have to be treated and then we have to wait—see how they do, and eventually they'll wake up on their own it just depends on how long that takes. I will send for someone to pick both of them up, and take them to the hospital. Right now we really have to go I'll bring your Dad I'll take care of him I promise." If there was one thing I could do I could trust David, and I knew he could help my friends.

"Okay I'll go . . . . just help them David."

"I will Anne." David walked up to the couch and picked up my Dad. I looked at Tyler and Tammy one last time.

"I'm so sorry."

We walked through the doorway—and onto the path through the gates. I looked up at the night sky the stars were amazing tonight, but in the back of my mind I knew I would never see the light of day ever again my heart was aching at the thought of that. Victor hadn't meant to turn me, but he still took everything away from me.

The car was still where we left it. David opened the door to the back seat and placed my Dad there he grabbed some blankets that were on the backseat floor and placed them over my Dads body. He closed the door and walked up to me—not saying a word his eyes were glowing again. He gave me a hug and kissed me on the forehead, he still looked amazing, even though his clothes were pretty damaged and extremely dirty he was my angel. David walked around the front of the car and took his place in the driver's seat—and I sat in the passenger seat not knowing what was going to happen to us.

As we took off I stared out the window—trying to count the stars I began to think about the many events that happened today. I couldn't believe I lost both my parents, and that both of my best friends were in a coma. I loved both of them so much my heart was broken for all of them I never got a chance to talk to my Dad about anything, and I ran away from my friends when all they wanted to do was help me. A tear ran down my cheek I wiped it away there was no use to cry it wouldn't help either of them. I knew I would never get a chance to talk to them ever again. A thought went through my mind I knew my Dad would be with my Mom, and they would be happy like they were before, but I would miss my Dad dearly I was spoiled not to be open with him, but it couldn't be fixed it was my fault.

The Funeral

I was burying my Dad today, and this time it was much different, because I wasn't human, all my senses were stronger than ever before I could feel the many emotions running through everyone which made the moment even sadder. I wanted to believe that the whole thing was just a nightmare, but I knew different my Dad was gone, and I knew life would be hard without him, but as I stood there I felt David's arm go through my arm and everything that I was feeling slipped away I knew that all I had was David to confide in which made me feel at ease, but a part of me knew that both Tammy and Tyler were in the hospital because of me I would never forgive myself for that.

David took care of everything for my friends they were on hourly observation, and getting the best treatment by the best Doctors he knew how important my friends were to me, and he would do anything in his power to make me feel at ease. I took a breath in and looked around the funeral home.

It was a small funeral, just me and David, and some people from my Dad's job. I didn't know what was going to happen to me, and David, but what I did know was that we could figure it out no matter what.

I kept thinking that both my parents were together now, and I wish I was with them, but it seemed that this was the only way my life would work out. Two lives to replace the one . . . . my life.

I knew I was going to miss my old life, but I knew I had to move on. It pained me to know that I would be leaving my parents here in this town, and my friends would wake up to find out that I was gone. It's kind of hard to know that I wouldn't die, but I guess it was fitting because I hated death so much it was my enemy and I knew it couldn't touch me now, not dying will be a struggle—complicated will be a major role in my life, but David seemed to uncomplicate most of it.

The funeral ended I couldn't watch my Dad be buried I was robbed of that I wanted so badly to go, but I knew the sun would kill me. I arranged for my Dad to be buried next to my Mom. I was left behind in the funeral home until night fall.

I left the funeral home and walked to Hill cemetery it would have been a long walk, but being a vampire made this walk feel like nothing. I finally made it to the heart of the cemetery I walked through the familiar gates I could feel the rain drops landing on my skin if I were human it would have bothered me, but I wasn't. It took me awhile to get to my parents tombstones I could smell the fresh earth.

"I'm so sorry Dad."

The thoughts of their life ran through my mind—happy memories of being a family and most of all the love they had for each other.

"Don't be sorry Anne." I turned around to see David leaning against the dead tree. It was deja vu to see him standing there again I shock my head in remembrance of that day, but I this time I wasn't an emotional mess. I let a sigh escape my lips.

"Oh but I am David I always will be." Before I knew it David was holding me in his arms.

"They never could be without each other could they David?"

David gently placed his hand under my chin, and forced me to look at him. "You're Mother and Father's love was to great Anne and when love is that great it can never truly be broken I think you, and I can understand that." A tear ran down my cheek David brushed it away softly.

"But it ended so tragically for them."

"As do all love stories do Anne—I'll take care of you for the rest of my life I promise you that."

"I know you will David." He looked at me and smiled he nodded and looked down again at my parents grave stones.

"I got you something Anne. He moved away from me and revealed his left hand from behind his back." A sob escaped my lips as he handed me his gift.

"Oh David it's beautiful." I raised the black rose to my nose and inhaled the sweet fragrance. I hugged David and kissed him softly. "I love you David."

"I love you to Anne I always have . . . . David slipped his hand into mine. Are you ready to go?" I looked at my parents graves for one last time then looked back at David.

"I'm ready." As we walked out of Hill cemetery I knew it wasn't over something told me that I would be hunted by my past for eternity this was an opening of a new chapter in my life a journey not yet written, but it was waiting to be written David and I would write it together . . . .